PRINCE OF KILLERS

A FOG CITY NOVEL

LAYLA REYNE

Cover Design: The Book Brander

Cover Photography: Wander Aguiar Photography

Editing: Edits by Kristi, Keren Reed Editing, Susie Selva

First Edition

June, 2019

E-Book ISBN: 978-1-7320883-6-8

Paperback ISBN: 978-1-7320883-7-5

Content Warnings: explicit sex including mild kink; explicit language; violence; instances and/or discussion of homophobia; off-page instances and/or discussion of PTSD, drug use, and abuse of minor characters.

ABOUT THIS BOOK

Get lost in the fog.

Hawes Madigan earned his reputation as the Prince of Killers.
Heir to criminal and corporate empires.
An assassin for hire in CEO's clothing.
Every day, he hates the moniker and his fate a little more.

Until sexy mysterious private investigator Dante Perry swaggers through his door.

Dante tells him what he suspects—there's a target on his back.
And makes him feel the unexpected, wild and free.
Like maybe he can change his fate. Like maybe he can be more.

But such a shift will require Hawes to root out the traitors in his organization.

And eliminate the one he unwittingly invited into his life. Assuming his heart and crown can survive the betrayals. Not to mention the bullets flying at his head.

There's no shortage of twists and turns in this first book of Hawes and Dante's M/M romantic suspense trilogy. Fair warning: buckle up, cliffhangers ahead!

To Allison,
who said I couldn't buy the pretties until I had a story. Ta-da!

ONE

Hawes clocked him the second he walked through the restaurant door. At first glance, and he was getting plenty of those, the striking man with long dark hair and leather bracelets could easily be mistaken for a rock star. Not uncommon for Restaurant Gary Danko, the local watering hole of San Francisco's elite. In the fog-shrouded hills of Fisherman's Wharf, the Michelin-starred restaurant with its elegant yet laid-back vibe attracted athletes, entertainers, tech kings, and financial wizards, as well as the city's political players and old-money families. Mr. Double Denim Rock God, with his long legs, windswept hair, and studded leather belt fit right in.

He carried himself like a rock star too, all loose-limbed and casually confident. All that was missing was the instrument, but a guitar slung over his back would be awfully inconvenient if Mr. Not A Rock God had to draw his real instrument of choice—the pistol tucked at the small of his back. Underneath a black tank and denim jacket, its impression was hardly noticeable, unless you were looking.

Hawes was always looking.

As was the chief of police sitting at the corner of the bar closest to the door. Braxton Kane moved quickly and discreetly, rotating on his stool and placing a hand on the stranger's right forearm, playing the odds that the man was right-handed. His bet was correct. The man instinctively jerked back with his dominant hand, but then he settled just as fast, his casual air returning in a blink. He exchanged a few words with Kane and withdrew a small leather case from his jacket pocket. He pulled out what looked like a business card—from Hawes's distance across the dining room—and handed it to Kane. The chief glanced at the card, and the wiry muscles of his army-honed body relaxed. He nodded toward Hawes's table, apparently giving the stranger the go-ahead.

Cop.

Hawes dismissed the thought as quickly as it had come. That gorgeous hair was the antithesis of regulation, his carriage was all wrong, and Kane hadn't recognized him. Neither had Hawes, and he made it a habit to regularly review the rosters of the local law enforcement agencies, SFPD and FBI included. The last thing he wanted to do was kill a LEO and upset the balance he'd spent the past five years rebuilding.

Merc was Hawes's next best guess, the same conclusion reached by the man and woman on either side of him, judging by the flash of metal barrels under the table.

"Safeties on," Hawes ordered, voice low. There was a crowded dining room full of innocents between the door and their corner booth. And Kane wouldn't have sent Canadian Tuxedo in his direction if he'd thought a shoot-out would ensue.

The man's long limbs remained loose as he approached; his core, however, did not, the gun against his spine a steadying rod. Or were his abs just that tight? Hawes could see their defined ridges through the fitted tank as the stranger drew near. He stopped on the other side of the table and braced his hands on top of the lone chair there. The lighter ends of his hair draped over his shoulders, and Hawes wanted to run his fingers through the strands. Wanted to curl them around his fist and see if all the shades of brown in his hair matched the many shades of rain-soaked earth in his eyes.

Hawes wanted a lot of things he didn't often get.

A name and explanation, though, he demanded. "Who are you?" No sense mincing words or introducing himself. The man obviously knew who Hawes was and had come here looking for him.

"Dante Perry." No Canadian accent to go with the double denim. Fucking shame. Though the rest of it made sense. Dark hair and eyes, long face, olive skin, and a pronounced Roman nose. Italian descent to go with the Italian name, and judging by his lack of accent, local. Or if he'd had an accent at one time, he'd since lost it or other-wise trained it out.

"What can I do for you, Mr. Perry?"

Dante pulled out the chair but paused before sitting, his keen eyes darting between the table and Hawes's compan-ions, as if he could see what their hands held beneath the white linen and lacquered wood. He shifted his gaze back to Hawes. "I don't plan to draw mine."

"Plans," Hawes said, skeptically. "All I've got is your name, Mr. Perry. I don't know that I trust you and your *plans*." He trusted Kane more, but better safe than sorry.

And he also demanded the show of respect. Commanded it.

Dante obliged. Hands on the table, where everyone could see them, he lowered himself into the chair. "I'm trusting you."

Hawes's gut clenched.

He ignored it and spread his arms over the back of the booth. A display of ease and confidence for their visitor, Kane, and anyone else watching. A signal for his associates to stand down, for the time being. Leverage, if Hawes needed to lift a leg and kick the table over, which would be another fucking shame. He hoped he wouldn't have to mess up Dante's handsome face. "All right, Mr. Perry, state your business."

Dante leaned forward, forearms resting on the table, and lowered his voice. "Someone in your organization wants to kill you."

Is that all?

Hawes laughed out loud, drawing curious looks from the nearby tables. Dante's eyes flashed with frustration, his scruff-covered jaw tightening to match.

"Not *my* organization," Hawes said, even as he mentally heard his sister chide, *Trap!* Their family hadn't survived at the top of the food chain for three generations by disclosing the full scope of their operations. Madigan Cold Storage was a legit business. They sold and shipped refrigeration units and frozen goods for more Bay Area restaurants, businesses, and fisheries than Hawes could count. It was also a legit euphemism.

"Not *yet*," Dante said. "How is Papa Cal?"

Hawes dropped his arms, and the safeties-off *snick* was unmistakable.

Dante raised his hands. "Don't shoot me for reading the news."

Fair point. Hawes's grandfather's declining health had first made news five years ago, when Callum Madigan's Alzheimer's had advanced enough to force him to step down as CEO of the family company, as well as from the various charities and local boards he sat on. Hawes had stepped into his shoes at twenty-eight, two years before he could even access the trust fund his deceased parents had left him. Reporters had come back around last month, when news had leaked that Pacific Heights's much beloved—and to a different segment of San Francisco, much feared—Papa Cal had been moved into a local hospice house for end-of-life care.

A leak, the origin of which Hawes's brother still couldn't hack.

"You know my family's business?"

Dante's eyes flicked again to the table and back up. Evidently so.

"Given the nature of our work," Hawes said, "I expect a disgruntled employee from time to time."

Translation: Running an organization of assassins, Hawes expected murder to cross the minds of his associates. That's what they were paid well for with respect to their contracted targets. With respect to Hawes, thinking about or wanting to kill him, their boss, was a natural hyperbolic gripe of any employee. Actually trying to kill him was a very different matter. There'd been no whiff of discontent arising to that level.

But the leak, of a fact known only among the top levels of the organization at the time, still rankled.

Dante drummed his fingers on the table. "I wonder if

one of those disgruntled employees knows what really happened to Isabelle Costa."

Hawes's blood ran cold. "Leave us," he ordered his associates. He braced a foot on the stand beneath the table-top, flip ready.

"No, don't." Dante stood, slowly, no sudden move-ments, and reached into his jacket pocket. He withdrew the card case Hawes had seen him handle earlier.

This close, Hawes could read *Dante* pressed into the leather on one side, and a time stamp—*23:01*—pressed into the other. The precise time was familiar, but Hawes couldn't place it, not when his attention was focused on the two business cards Dante placed on the table. He slid the first one to Hawes, thumb and index finger pressing firmly on the corners. *Dante Perry, Private Investigator*, the plain ecru card read, with a local post office box, phone number, and email address.

"Run my prints, check me out, then call me when you're ready to talk human resources." He pushed the second card across the table. "Call her if you need more than your brother's exhaustive background checks. She'll vouch for me."

Hawes forced himself not to react. *This* card had no doubt been the one Dante had given Kane. It was a card Hawes carried in his own wallet.

"I'll look for your call." Confident, Dante turned and swaggered toward the exit like a rock star, as if he didn't know two pistols were aimed at him. But the private inves-tigator did know, and he didn't care. He knew Hawes would call.

And he was right. No matter the background checks or references, Hawes would make contact. Because Dante

Perry had walked into this restaurant tonight, into Hawes's life, and resurrected his worst nightmare.

Hawes kept his foot braced on the pole beneath the table until Dante cleared the door.

"Follow him," he ordered Jodie. "But be back in ten. We're on the clock."

She nodded, slipped out of the booth, and glided across the dining room on silver stilettos, a flash of violet lamé hustling the same direction Dante had departed.

"Can I put a soufflé in the oven for you, Mr. Madigan?"

Hawes's attention snapped to the waiter approaching his table and to Kane passing behind him. Catching Hawes's eye, Kane tilted his head toward the restrooms and continued walking in that direction.

"Not tonight, thank you," Hawes answered the waiter. He hoped his smile didn't look as forced as it felt. Everyone here was always so good to him, but his mind was now a million miles away from the dinner he'd enjoyed. And he was expected elsewhere. Yet courtesy was still owed, as his grandmother had drilled into him. "Cheese course did me in," he added with a pat to his belly. A compliment for all involved. "I think the check is all I have room for."

The waiter smiled, pleased. "Right away, sir."

Hawes tossed his napkin onto the table and fished out his wallet. "Pay the check and bring the car around," he said to Ray, his other associate, as he shoved a stack of bills into his hand.

Ray cut his eyes to the restroom hallway, reading Hawes's intent. "It's not wise."

"I didn't ask you."

"At least let me go with you. It's my job."

"Your job is to be my backup on the contract we're executing tonight. You are not here for my protection, which in any event, is unnecessary where Kane is concerned." Hawes pocketed his wallet, pulled out his phone, and carefully tucked the two cards Dante had left behind into the card compartment on the back. "Text me when the car is out front. I don't want to be late."

He slid out of the booth before Ray could object further. Hawes was confident in his hand-to-hand abilities against Kane, and he was equally confident it would never come to that with the chief.

Kane was waiting for him inside the otherwise empty men's room. Wise choice; no cameras or recording devices in here. Being seen dining at the same establishment or exchanging pleasantries at a charity or veterans' event was one thing; secret meetings were another. Potentially damning, for both their reputations.

"You didn't know him?" Hawes asked without preamble.

"I didn't." Kane flashed the same card Hawes now had in his pocket. "But he checks out with Cruz."

Saved Hawes the call, but he'd still have Holt run the background checks and Dante's prints. He'd dropped too big a bomb to ignore. "Have you heard of him *at all*?"

Kane shook his head. "He wasn't on my radar." He dug a caramel candy out of his pocket, peeled off the golden wrapper, and popped it into his mouth. "You gonna tell me what he wanted?"

"He told me someone wanted to kill me."

Kane laughed, same as Hawes had. "Is it a day that ends in *y*?"

"Exactly."

"But that only explains your bark of laughter." Kane leaned back against the vanity, hands braced on either side of his narrow hips, fingers curled around the sink's porcelain lip. "Perry said something else that made you and your fire team go on alert. You gonna tell me what that was?"

Of course the top cop had picked up on the abrupt change in mood.

"No," Hawes answered. Not until he knew more about Dante's motives and his connection to Isabelle. No sense unleashing that ghost on anyone else if it turned out to be just that—a ghost, whose haunting was limited to Hawes. A specter that had reared its head periodically over the past three years but never gained form enough to torture anyone but him.

"Didn't figure you would." Kane hung his head, and Hawes wondered how much one Madigan or another had contributed to the chief's thinning hairline. His high and tight buzz cut disguised it from most, but Hawes had seen pictures of the before and the reality of the after.

"Safer for you, Brax."

The chief lifted a hand, then his hazel eyes. "I know the drill. Just give me a warning if things are about to go tits-up."

Hawes cringed. "You know I hate that saying, right?"

"You know I spent two decades in the military, right?"

The heavy mood eased with their laughter. Kane's sense of humor, his sass, and his loyalty when it mattered most—a promise he'd never wavered from—were the underpinnings of this unlikely alliance. That and his willingness to look the other way as long as Hawes kept his promises too. "Yes, Chief Kane, I will let you know if the shit is about to hit the fan."

Kane rolled his eyes. "Because that phrase is so much better." He pushed off the sink and started for the door. "Keep me posted, and stay safe." Hand on the knob, he paused and glanced back. All trace of humor was gone from his eyes. "All of you."

TWO

Hawes didn't have time to linger on Kane's words, as his phone vibrated with a text from Ray. **At the curb.**

On my way, he texted back.

But first, he tipped Dante's business card out of his phone case and into his other palm. Handling it carefully, he snapped a couple of quick photos and shot them off to Holt with a message to commence digging.

Copy that, his twin replied.

Hawes tucked the card back into the case, pocketed his phone, and headed for the exit. Outside, Jodie was standing next to the idling Benz.

Shit. She'd lost Dante.

"Sorry, boss," she said as Hawes slid into the back seat. "He made a loop around the block and hopped on the fucking cable car."

No way would she have made it back in the ten minutes Hawes had allowed if she'd followed Dante onto one of those. Also, "fucking cable car" was right.

"It's fine," Hawes said. "Holt's on him."

That would have to satisfy, including Hawes's mind, if he was going to be sharp for the job ahead. Granted, all he had to do was press a button, but he could never be too careful, especially when explosives were involved. There was only one other method of assassination Hawes hated more, but while he was confident foregoing a pistol, he wouldn't ask that of his operatives. "Are we set?" he asked.

Jodie nodded. "Lucas texted. All wired up."

Tension rippled through Hawes, tightening his insides. He didn't let it show. "The area is clear?"

"Pier's deserted except for the warehouse." The derelict pier was set to be demolished later that month. They were doing the city a favor, taking down the largest of the remaining structures on it, but they had to be sure no one was in it.

"You're certain the women are out?"

"All of them." Ray shifted in his seat and passed a tablet to Hawes, two windows open on-screen. "The left one is the security loop Holt hijacked." Everything looked normal in that window. Two guards sat at a card table eating soup out of sourdough bread bowls. "The right window is the real footage from an hour ago." The guards' faces were planted in their food. "Avery got the women out and onto the boat while Lucas wired the place."

"Reno will be by for his nightly check-in at ten," Jodie said, "and find his precious 'merchandise' gone." She sneered at the term the cartel transporter used time and again to refer to the trafficking victims he regularly traded in. The warehouse was a layover stop. The only one Reno had left after Jodie and Ray had taken out a winemaker who was letting Reno use his cellars to hide women awaiting transport.

Hawes scrolled through the live surveillance feeds. No sign of activity inside or outside the warehouse. "Only two guards?" Hawes expected more firepower after the winery incident last week.

"Reno thinks he's flying under the radar with this one," Ray said. "Doesn't want to draw attention to it."

Clearly, neither Reno nor his guards knew Holt had tapped into their webcam. Served them right for broadcasting the "fun" they had with their victims. Not that the trafficking alone hadn't earned them vetted status. These were the kind of contracts Hawes wanted for the organization. Gray areas and despicable human beings the law couldn't reach or catch—the Madigans could.

Jodie turned the car down the road to the pier. The street was almost pitch-black toward the end, the city no longer maintaining the doomed stretch. It was a perfect, under the radar hideout for the cartel's trafficking operation, until they'd been put on Hawes's radar. The tablet vibrated in his hands, indicating they were within range for the remote detonation app. Jodie wheeled the car around and backed it into a narrow alley between two smaller, boarded-up structures, out of sight for when Reno drove past.

"We should be good to go," Jodie said.

Hawes's insides went from tight to knotted as his mind flashed back to another dark night three years ago. To the unintended death precipitated by the weapon of destruction he wielded tonight. He had to be sure.

He cycled through the surveillance feeds one more time. All clear. He moved the monitoring window to the side of the tablet and brought the detonation app to the front. Thumb over the Activate trigger, he'd hit it as soon as Reno was inside. Far enough in to guarantee his death, but before he realized something was amiss.

Motion in the other window caught Hawes's eye.

"Shit!" He dragged that window back to the center and zoomed in. There, on the edge of view, a man crouched and peered into one of the compartments where Reno had hidden the women. "There's still someone inside. Looks like he's checking for the women."

He flashed the tablet at Ray, who likewise muttered a curse.

"He's probably one of Reno's men."

"*Probably* isn't good enough," Hawes said, even if the man did have a gun holstered on his hip. Hawes had been wrong before; he wouldn't risk it again. Those were the rules now—his rules. He dialed Holt from the tablet.

It rang once through the car's speakers before Holt picked up. "I see him too. Facial recognition is running."

"Call Lucas," Hawes told Ray. "Have him walk you through *exactly* what he did to clear the building."

Ray shoved open the door. "On it."

Phone to his ear, he paced in front of the Benz while Hawes and Jodie waited for Holt's update. On-screen, the man in the warehouse gave the two dead men a wide berth as he continued to check the holding cells.

"Scout for Reno?" Jodie asked.

"Possibly," Hawes said. "Or for a rival cartel, or a fed. Coast Guard has both been snooping around this case too."

"Strike out here," Holt said. "Facial recognition didn't ping."

Ray braced a hand on the frame of the open car door. "Lucas is certain there was no one else in or around the warehouse when he and Avery cleared out with the women."

"Reno's five minutes out," Holt said, adding to their mounting complications.

The biggest one was in that warehouse. They needed to flush him out and confirm who he worked for. "Holt, activate the comm devices. Give us Reno's location every ninety seconds." Hawes lowered the armrest between the back seats and opened the custom-built, foam-lined "tool case" inside. "Ray, you take the north entry. Jodie, you've got the south side." He handed each operative an over-ear comm and hooked on his own. "I'll come through the front. We herd him toward the center, then out the back."

"Toward the water?" Jodie said. "We'll be cut off too if we don't get him out before Reno gets here."

"There's enough of the promenade left for you to skirt around the building," Holt said. "Security feed shows it's clear. As soon as you get out of the blast radius, I'll detonate the explosives from here."

Assuming they booked it fast enough to do so before Reno caught on to the trap. This was risky, but risking an innocent life was unacceptable. Hawes untucked the garrote from the case's foam and lowered the lid with a *snap*. "We wait for Reno and kill him if we have to. So long as the explosion goes off in the end, the evidence will be destroyed and it'll be linked to the winery explosion, as intended." It would look like the cartel was cleaning up their own mess.

"Worse comes to worst," Hawes added, "we'll have the water."

"That water's freezing," Ray protested.

"Better than burning alive."

And better than living with more innocent blood on his hands.

"Reno's two blocks out."

Holt's report came just as their hiccup stepped into Hawes's reach. The man had been so busy yammering on his phone about the *merchandise*—a scout, then; not an innocent—that he hadn't realized he'd been expertly redirected by Ray and Jodie, who'd been locking some doors and opening others. Or that Hawes was hiding in the shadows right behind him.

"He's all yours, boss," Jodie spoke quietly from her position on the other side of the main room's entry door. Ready to round it at any second.

Hawes slowly separated the two ends of the garrote, minimizing the *hiss* of the wire as he unfurled it. No dramatics needed. He inched a wingtip out of the shadows and shifted his weight to step forward.

The scout spoke a name, and Hawes immediately retreated.

"Fuck!" Holt murmured, having heard the same thing. "Stay right there and keep him close. I'm tapping into his wireless signal. I'll check it against their list."

"What's going on?" Ray whispered.

"Rival cartel," Holt answered, since Hawes could not.

"Acceptable collateral," Jodie said.

No such thing.

And the rival cartel was not their target. This was not a war Hawes wanted to set off. Yes, war was likely inevitable if the rival cartel was willing to consider such a rip-off, but for Kane's sake, Hawes wouldn't be the one to start it. Didn't mean he'd let this guy get away, or not get his actual target.

"Confirmed," Holt said. "Abort?"

"No," Hawes said, at full voice, intentionally. "Capture."

"What?" The scout whipped around. "Who's there?"

Hawes lunged out of the shadows. "Bad night to plan a rip-off."

The scout reached for his gun, but Hawes, moving faster, flung one end of the garrote toward the crook of the scout's right elbow. The wire looped around, hooked, and Hawes yanked, stopping the scout short of grabbing his weapon. The man cocked back his left arm, preparing to swing. Hawes ducked, and Jodie swept in from the scout's blindside, grabbing his raised elbow and his gun.

"Good luck with that," she said with a lethal smile.

She jerked the scout's arm the opposite direction as Hawes, who was still holding his right arm trapped in the garrote. The *pop* of dislocating shoulders made Hawes cringe. Add to that the *thump* of knees hitting concrete— Ray kicking the scout's legs out from behind him—and even Holt groaned in sympathy over the comms.

Victory, however, was short-lived. Holt turned serious again in an instant. "Reno's at the gate."

The scout gasped and grunted as Jodie finished trussing him up. "Who the fuck are you guys?"

Hawes knelt and got in his face, making sure the man got a good look at him. "They call me the Prince of Killers." He hated the moniker, whispered through the foggy under-belly of San Francisco's disreputable elite. Hated how it came to be and what it implied, but there was no denying its implication was useful in certain circumstances. Like now, as fear widened the scout's eyes. Hawes also needed deterrence to penetrate his brain. "Remind your cartel boss who keeps the order in Fog City. Don't fuck with it. And *you* remember who saved your life tonight."

"Saved my life?"

"I'm not leaving you here for Reno to find, or to die. That's a war none of us needs." He stood and turned to Jodie and Ray. "Toss him in the Bay."

"I'll drown like this," the scout hissed.

"Better hope you float," Ray said as he hefted him over his shoulder.

The scout continued to struggle as they exited via the promenade. When the inky water of the Bay was in sight, he tried bargaining. "I'll tell you whatever you want to know."

"I'm not interested in anything you have to say." But Hawes did know a certain Bureau AD who was investigating the cartel's trafficking operations. A little goodwill could go a long way. "But I know someone who might be."

THREE

An hour later, the waterfront was still alight, the fire from the explosion raging, and the fleet of emergency vehicles casting their bright lights on the scene. A stark contrast to the occasional car that passed by Hawes in the midtown residential neighborhood where he'd arranged the hand-off of the scout. Hawes dragged his gaze from the fiery sight, the last such explosion he ever intended to set, and hoofed it up the hill. As much as he would have liked to call it a night, he needed to return to the family fort and debrief with his brother and sister. Needed to find out what Holt, now freed from mission-comm duty, had dug up on Dante Perry.

Ray stood at the mouth of an alley half a block up the hill, backlit by the glare of headlights, fog swirling around his legs. Jodie edged the Benz's nose out from between the two structures on either side of the narrow street.

"Take me to the house," Hawes said, turning into the alley.

Mind whirring over Dante, Hawes almost missed the car reversing direction, the taillights reflecting brighter off the house at the other end of the alley, the side-view mirror appearing on the edge of his periphery, the rear door handle moving out of his reach.

Ray's footsteps closed in fast and loud behind him.

Hawes spun, expecting to see someone chasing them into the alley, only to find Ray's pistol raised and aimed directly at him. Hawes stumbled back a step, struggling to put the pieces together. "What the fuck?"

Ray's eyes held his. They were not the eyes of an ally. Not those of the man who'd fought by Hawes's side just an hour ago. They were cold, intent on death. What the hell was going on?

Hawes patted his pocket for the garrote. Empty. His stomach sank.

Ray grinned menacingly. "Missing something?" The garrote dangled from the fingertips of his free hand.

"Have you lost your mind?"

"Better question is, have you?" Ray tossed the garrote behind him, toward the street, then charged forward.

Hawes didn't have time to think. Didn't have time to dwell on the boulder of betrayal threatening to flatten him. All he had time to do was react. He ducked, and Ray's gun crashed into the driver's-side window. Glass rained down onto the pavement, crunching under Hawes's feet as he spun and rammed a shoulder into Ray's middle.

"So much for doing your job," Hawes said. "You call this protection?"

"Not my job," Ray grunted. "Said it yourself."

"Neither is killing me."

"Except it is." Ray brought the butt of his gun down on

Hawes's back, dead center and hard as hell, two hundred pounds of muscle behind it.

A spike to his spine, the hit sent waves of pain radiating out to all of Hawes's limbs. He let loose a shout, then gritted his teeth against the agony, against the urge to drop to the ground and curl into a ball. That would only lead to death. He was sure of that. Dante's earlier prediction echoed loudly in his head. Fighting through the pain with a roar, he shoved Ray with all his strength, enough to get a foot of separation. Enough to avoid another pistol whip, hike up his elbow, and ram it under Ray's chin. With his attacker's head flung back, Hawes kicked a leg up between Ray's spread ones, foot aimed directly at the traitor's crotch.

Ray howled, bent forward, and struggled to right himself, hands coming down to shield himself from another kick. Hawes got there first, landing a second kick to his middle. "Consider that your severance pay," he said, as the traitor stumbled backward out of the alley. A blaring car horn warned of Ray's impending fate if he didn't regain his balance soon.

But Ray was no longer the focus of Hawes's attention.

The driver's-side door was flung open and jammed against the siding of the adjacent house, the rest of the broken glass from the window—and from Jodie's skirt—tinkling to the asphalt. It crunched under her heels, but not as ominously as the safety-off snick of her gun or the whoosh of air around the knife she flipped in her other hand.

Not just a single boulder—a fucking landslide of betrayal walloped Hawes. He fought to remain standing. Forced himself to shake out his limbs and prepare for round two. "You too? Did you even bother to follow Perry earlier?"

"Perry's not my concern."

"I can see that." Hawes could also see, with one quick glance at the car, that he was trapped. The Benz was practically parked on the opposite curb, making too narrow an opening for even Hawes to squeeze through. He could use the bars on the left building's subfloor windows to vault onto the trunk, then scramble over the top of the car, but Ray was still stumbling around on the sidewalk and Jodie would land a shot before Hawes could finish executing those maneuvers.

Through it was, then, and since Hawes wouldn't carry a gun and Ray had thrown his best weapon the opposite direction, speed, distraction, and sharp elbows were the only options he had left.

"Were you and Ray planning to make your move tonight, or did Perry accelerate your timeline?"

"Got orders to let you burn," Jodie said. "Turns out that scout saved you too. For an extra hour."

She and Ray had been doing a job. They'd been hired to kill him. Someone hadn't merely wanted to kill him. They'd enacted a plan to do just that. Dante had been more right than he probably knew.

"Orders from whom?" he asked Jodie.

He didn't expect an answer, but with each word he spoke, Hawes stepped closer to where three wires broke off from the dozen or so cables running horizontally along the building's exterior. He couldn't yank the whole bunch off the wall, secured as they were by bolted-in loops, but he could rip free those three vertical-running cords.

More weapons.

"Not to sound arrogant," Hawes said, inching closer, "but I find it hard to believe you found a better boss."

"You do sound arrogant." Jodie spun the hilt of the knife in her hand, her hold loose and flexible. Ready to grip and throw in an instant, like Hawes's sister had taught her.

Panic streaked through Hawes, sudden and breathtaking.

If Jodie and Ray had moved on him tonight, was someone else moving on Helena? On Holt and his wife and daughter? Was this a coordinated attack on the family? A coup? Or was he the only target? Whipping out his phone and calling home wasn't an option. Neither was asking the question. He didn't want to put that idea, if it wasn't already there, in the head of whoever was behind this.

"Can't say I'm not disappointed. You were one of the best, Jodie."

"I am the best."

She proved it the next second, catching the knife mid-spin and hurling it at him, the action practiced and deadly. His quick reflexes and slender frame saved him from a direct hit, the knife slicing through the gray silk of his suit sleeve and flying past his rotated shoulder. She didn't wait to attack, following directly in the knife's wake, aiming to take advantage of Hawes's momentary distraction and open body position. He shot out his left hand, yanked the wires off the wall, and spun into her charging body, forcing her to try to wrap herself around him. He jammed his elbow into her side, and the slight bend in her stance was enough for Hawes to loop the wires over her head and around her neck. She flailed, limbs trying to land a strike, but she'd already used her best weapon for that. The knife was a good two feet away on the ground, and the gun in her other hand was too much of a risk given their close quarters. Cables still clutched in his hands—ignoring the sting of the wires digging into his palms—Hawes used the window bars to vault up onto the trunk of the car and jump back down behind Jodie, his legs tucked for maximum momentum on his way to the ground.

Jodie's neck snapped, her gun clattered to the ground, and her body followed with a muffled *thump*.

"Madigan, get down!" came a shout from the far end of the alley.

Hostile or friendly, Hawes couldn't say, but he didn't think twice about heeding the warning. He snatched up Jodie's knife, stepped back, and yanked open the rear door, crouching between it and the open driver's door. A bullet whizzed overhead, and Hawes whipped around, staring through the frame of the broken window. An apparently recovered Ray was recovered no more. Blood bloomed from a bull's-eye hit to his chest. He crumpled to the ground on the other side of the car door Hawes knelt behind.

Light flooded the alley from the direction the warning had come, and Hawes spun again. On the second-level porch of the house at the end of the alley, Dante stepped into the glow cast by the porch light. He was the last person Hawes expected to see again tonight, and gun in hand, stance professional, he looked as far from Mr. Rock God as possible. "This way!" he shouted, waving Hawes in his direction.

"What the fuck are you doing here?"

Dante's eyes flickered to Jodie. "When she didn't tail me past the corner, I knew something was off."

"Have you been following us all night?"

"Most of it, yes. Now let's fucking go!"

Go where? "It's a dead end that way."

"It's not." Dante raised his firing arm, and Hawes flipped the knife in his hand, ready to throw, but Dante's next words made it clear he was gesturing toward the street. "But that way is. Between the car horns and the gunshot, SFPD will be here any minute."

Hawes glanced at the two bodies on the ground. "I can't just leave them here." And he couldn't leave with a stranger he hardly knew, no matter who vouched for him. But could he stay?

"You were last seen alone," Dante said. "No one knows you met back up with them." He gestured at Ray and Jodie. "When the cops come calling, claim it was a dispute between them, or with a third-party who got away."

"My prints are all over the place."

"On your car, that's expected. Are you hurt? Bleeding?"

Hawes checked himself over. His back hurt like a bitch, but he hadn't been shot or nicked. He flipped over his hands. The wires had left deep grooves in his palms. He didn't think the skin was broken, but he couldn't be sure, as red as they were. "Maybe these," he said, holding up his hands. While they were lifted, he checked the area around him. No blood on the ground or elsewhere. "Would just be on the wires."

"Use the knife to cut the portion—"

"Don't tell me how to do my job," Hawes said, already hacking through the cables. He pocketed the cut portions and used his sleeve to wipe down the dangling ends and the wall, removing any fingerprints. "The bullet from your gun?"

"Won't be traced."

Car tires squealed close by, accompanied by sirens.

"Madigan!" Dante shouted. "We gotta go. Now!"

This was not the best idea, but as the sirens grew louder, Hawes was out of options. He jumped over Jodie's body and sprinted for the stairs at the end of the alley, taking them two at a time. At the top, Dante grabbed his hand... and dragged him over the wooden stair rail.

The free fall didn't last more than a couple of seconds, but it felt like the longest two seconds of Hawes's life. He'd almost died in that alley—twice—but aside from his initial second of surprise, at no other time had the situation been out of his control. Falling through the dark night, Dante's hand the only thing holding him to reality, was not being in control. It was further from control, and reality, than Hawes had been in a long time.

At three seconds, his back hit canvas. He dipped, then was flung back in the air, his hand ripped from Dante's. A smaller fall followed, then another, before Hawes realized they'd landed on a trampoline.

"Let's go!" Dante whisper-shouted as he scrambled off.

Hawes followed, hopping off the trampoline and onto the ground in what appeared to be a shared backyard. "You could have told me before we jumped that I wasn't going to die."

"Can't make that promise yet." Gun drawn, back pressed against the closest building, Dante peeked around the corner.

Blue lights flashed down the narrow exit walk, and sirens screamed by on the street as police cruisers sped to the alley on the opposite side of the yard. They had to move, now.

Hawes snatched up the knife he'd dropped mid-fall and followed Dante, the two of them creeping down the dark walkway. A few feet shy of the street, Dante paused and tucked his gun back into his waistband where Hawes had first noticed it earlier that night. Not more than two hours ago, and yet the world had turned upside down in that short amount of time.

And it kept turning. Dante rotated to face him and held out his hand expectantly. "The knife," he demanded. "You can't go running out into the street with it, and as attractive as that fitted suit is on you, there's nowhere to hide that blade that won't be obvious."

Hawes hesitated, unwilling to give up his sole tactical weapon to the man with a gun and a good thirty pounds on him.

"I trusted you at the restaurant earlier," Dante said, as if reading his thoughts. "And I gave you information that proved to be true. Now I need you to trust me." Here in the shadows, his big dark eyes were bottomless black holes. Dangerous celestial objects with enough gravitational force to draw Hawes in and snuff him out for good. Hawes already felt the pull to this stranger who'd told him the truth and saved his life.

He handed over the knife. "I need to get to my brother and sister."

Dante strapped the knife into an ankle holster under his pant leg next to another blade. "I can get you there." He righted himself and led them out of the shadows and onto the sidewalk. "But there's a catch."

"What kind of catch?" Hawes asked, walking close at his side.

"How do you feel about riding tandem?"

Hawes followed the direction of Dante's fond gaze to a rainbow parade of fiberglass crotch-rockets. Surely not. No

—there, right at the end, pearlescent midnight-blue and gleaming chrome… "The Harley?"

Dante smirked. "The Harley."

Hawes's gut clenched, again. Damn, this was gonna be a thing.

FOUR

Hawes had grown up in San Francisco, had been born and bred in its hills and valleys. He'd learned at an early age how to turn a car's wheels when parked on a slope and how to perfectly time the release of the clutch and the press of the gas so as not to roll the wrong way down Jones Street. He would never, however, get used to cruising his hometown's hills on a motorcycle, not his sister's and certainly not Dante Perry's. And he most definitely would not get used to riding tandem, when one wrong bump could jostle him loose and send him flailing to his death.

By the time they rumbled onto the stone drive of the sage-green Victorian with its high-pitched roofs and bright-white trim, Hawes had mentally uttered more Hail Marys than he had the Sunday after he'd blown the homecoming king. He wished he could say he'd been holding tight to Dante as an excuse to map out every nook and cranny of his ripped torso, but regrettably, he hadn't thought beyond a death grip for survival until after he'd climbed off the bike. At which point, managing to stand on his embarrassingly unsteady legs took precedence. *Assassinate people for a living, no problem. Run a multimillion-dollar company before age thirty, can do. Ride a motorcycle in San Francisco, fuck no.*

He gingerly curled one hand into a fist and leaned with his knuckles against the knotted cypress next to the driveway. By contrast, Dante the Confident dismounted the bike with the same casual ease he'd displayed all night. Hawes admired and hated him. The latter was easier to speak too, sarcasm as good a weapon as any. "Did you really think a Hog was the best idea here?"

"It was my dad's," Dante said, stealing another of Hawes's weapons. "He taught me to ride a bike on these hills long before I learned to drive a car on them." He slid a hand over Hawes's lower back, the weight more steadying than it had any right to be. "Never been on a bike?"

"I have," Hawes answered. "Sister's Ducati. Not my favorite thing."

"You don't say." There was humor in Dante's eyes, and also heat, same as in his touch. If Hawes didn't know any better—

"Take your hand off him."

Dante instantly dropped his hand. Hawes felt the loss almost as keenly as the earlier blow to his back, which was making itself known again now that fear and adrenaline were wearing off.

"You good?" Dante asked, not touching him but remaining close.

"Yes." *No,* but it was better to lie than agitate the owner of the cool, crisp voice that had sliced through the darkness.

"I'm fine, Hena," Hawes called up toward the house. He didn't need to look to know his sister was waiting on her perch, back to one of the porch columns, legs stretched out in front of her, tonight's weapon of choice—Ka-Bar or Sig Sauer—resting on her thigh. Hawes hoped her fingers hadn't twitched too much at the slip of her nickname.

"You can leave now," she said to Dante.

"I'm not leaving until he's home safely."

"He is home."

Hawes cleared his throat. "I don't think that's what—" His interjection was cut off by a flash of black leather, pale skin, and long blonde hair as Helena vaulted off the porch and landed in front of them.

"I know what he meant, Big H." Barefoot, knees absorbing the minimal impact her petite frame made, Helena had landed quiet as a cat, barely making a sound. She rarely ever did. Silent and deadly was her specialty, and right then, her ice-blue eyes were glaring daggers at Dante. "And he's not your concern." She spun the knife in her hand, like Jodie had earlier, and a shiver raced up Hawes's spine.

"Go," he said to Dante, sensing Helena on a precipice. She'd obviously gotten wind of what had happened in the alley, no doubt also knew about the complication at the warehouse, and had gone into hyperprotective mode. "Go," he repeated when Dante hesitated. Dark eyes swung to his, and Hawes held his gaze, projecting the confidence that tonight's events had dulled. Now at home, or rather, the home he'd grown up in, he was determined to wrestle things back under his control. "I've got this, and I've got your number."

"Use it." Dante pivoted and swaggered back to his bike.

In the restaurant earlier, when Dante had walked away from his table, Hawes had been distracted by unknowns, debating whether the PI was friend or foe. He still wasn't sure, but this time, it didn't distract Hawes from checking out Dante's ass. It filled out a pair of Levi's nicely, no debate there. Dante threw a leg over the bike, straddling the seat, and Hawes cursed himself again for not enjoying the ride more.

"Nine out of ten," Helena whispered at his side. "Grabbable for sure." She bit her bottom lip, humming with approval, and made a squeezing motion with her free hand.

Hawes breathed easier. "What's it take for a ten out of ten?"

"Need to see it out of the jeans." She bumped his shoulder. "But I'm guessing you're calling dibs on that."

The Harley roared to life, and Dante shot him a parting smirk. He was sexier than he had any right to be in double denim, that rock-star hair streaming in the wind behind him. Yeah, Hawes called dibs.

And besides... "What happened to Danielle?" Hawes asked as they started up the steps.

Helena shrugged one shoulder.

"Or Eric?"

She shrugged the other.

No one was ever good enough for his little sister. Or maybe she didn't think she was good enough for them. Though that would be ridiculous. She was gorgeous, a talented lawyer by day, and there was no one Hawes would rather have by his side in a fight at night. Anyone would be lucky to have her, but whoever that person was, they'd never have all of her.

Something Hawes understood all too well. Not everyone got lucky like their parents and grandparents, or like Holt and Amelia. His own bedmates had come and gone, frustrated that Hawes was holding back. For their protection, and his family's. But there was always a red line that separated him from his lovers. He hadn't bothered to toe that line recently, staying far away from it by sticking to one-night stands and club hookups. Dante, however, knew who he was, knew about their family and the business behind their business.

"Brax called," Helena said, confirming the heads-up Hawes had suspected.

"And?" Hawes prompted.

"Told him you were already home." She grinned over her shoulder as she pushed open the front door. "Better go get our stories straight before he gets here to see for himself."

Hawes hissed through clenched teeth as the cold lidocaine cream tickled the abraded skin of his palms. The wires hadn't broken the skin, just left deep, angry grooves, but professional examination, treatment, and bandaging by their very own surgical nurse was insisted upon. He grunted his displeasure all around.

"Oh, come on." His sister-in-law's green eyes twinkled. "I've patched you up from far worse injuries."

"Like that knife wound to your left shoulder," Helena said from where she sat across the table.

Hawes flinched in remembered pain, then flinched

again as very real pain rippled out from his throbbing back. "The knife wound *you* gave me?"

Helena paused in her petting of the family's giant Siberian cat to blow him a kiss. Amelia's demeanor, however, was no longer joking. She rested a hip against the dining room table next to him. "Fess up, Big H. Where else are you injured?"

He contemplated lying, but this was the person who, when she wasn't on duty at the hospital, tortured answers out of the organization's targets. Who eight months ago had pushed a ten-pound baby out of her willowy, five-foot-eight frame. Amelia scared him almost as much as Helena did.

"Took a pistol whip to the back." He held out his index finger, pretending it was his spine, and with his other fist, mimicked Ray bringing the gun down on it.

Cringing, Helena shifted in her chair, and Daisy skittered off her lap, joining the tabby, Tulip, in the corner to play.

"I'm going to need to check your back," Amelia told him.

He nodded and tried to extricate himself from his jacket, cursing as he made his back ache worse.

"Easy," Amelia said. "Let me help."

Out of his jacket, Hawes unbuttoned his wrinkled dress shirt far enough to lower it to his elbows, exposing most of his back.

Amelia rotated him sideways on the chair and stepped fully behind him. "Ouch!" she rightly assessed. "That's gonna hurt like a bitch tomorrow." Again, spot on, Nurse Madigan.

As her fingertips gently probed the injured area, Hawes

distracted himself with the purpose Helena had mentioned on their way up the steps outside. "Basics," he said, holding up his bandaged hands. "How do I explain these to Kane?"

Helena reached into Amelia's toolbox full of medical supplies and took out a roll of bandages. She tore off two strips and wrapped one around each of her hands, tucking the loose ends under her palms. "Combat practice."

"Or you were amusing Lily," Amelia said. "Baby girl got a cut on her hand today."

Hawes whipped his head around. "She okay?"

"She's fine. Just a scrape." Amelia swatted his shoulder. "Stop being the overprotective uncle."

Chuckling, he looked down again at his hands, then over at Helena's. "As likely an excuse— *Fuck!*" Hawes cursed as Amelia prodded the exact right—or wrong—spot on his back. "I'd say you found it."

"Stay," Amelia ordered him, like she would her crawling daughter, and disappeared into the adjacent kitchen.

Left alone in the dining room with Helena, Hawes bore the full brunt of his sister's icy-eyed glare. "I'm waiting for an explanation," she said.

"I'd prefer to give it just once."

"Fine. I'll holler for Holt to come down."

"No, you won't," Amelia said, reentering the room. "He's in the zone."

"Lily's knocked out, then?" Hawes said.

"Like a light." Amelia smiled the smile of a happy mother. It grew wider as she showed off her bounty—a Ziploc of ice and a baby sling. "We'll go to them."

Ten minutes later, the bag of ice strapped to his back

with the bright pink sling, Hawes followed Helena and Amelia upstairs. At the second-floor landing, he noticed only one side of the floor was lit, the multicolored glass from Helena's Tiffany lamps casting a kaleidoscope of color on the common area walls and luring the cats away from their feet. His grandparents' master on the opposite end of the floor was dark.

"Rose?" he asked after their grandmother.

"With Papa Cal," Helena said.

Hawes had figured as much. They hadn't seen much of Rose since they'd moved Cal into hospice. Hawes made a mental note to stop by tomorrow. They continued on to the third floor—Holt's family's domain—and from the seating area there, up the spiral staircase to Holt's lair.

And *lair* was the right word for it.

At the very top of the house, in the peaks of the roof, the attic bonus room stretched the length of the structure. During the day, sun streamed in through the arched front window and overhead skylights. At night it was just as bright, owing to the tech-geek wall of wonder. Across the long, uninterrupted wall, LCD screens were stacked three high and four wide and served as monitors for Holt's bank of computers and surveillance feeds. Each of their family's homes and all their business operations, the legal and illegal ones, could be observed from this perch. It was everything Holt needed to be the eyes and ears of the organization and to do what he did best—digital assassination: financial, social, and otherwise. All from the comfort of home so he could spend time with his daughter.

And that's where this perch diverged from the one Holt had at the company's headquarters. Lily's presence here couldn't be missed—from the wooden crib beneath the front window, to the golden bear mobile twirling above it, to the rocking chair in the corner. It destroyed the typical hacker vibe, but it also humanized the place, more than Holt's wall of monitors and old military-style cot ever had.

Amelia crossed the room to her husband, gave him a kiss on the cheek, and peered into the crib, which had been rolled closer to Holt's seat at the computers. The *tap-tap-tap* of his rapid-fire typing was the best trick they'd discovered for getting Lily to sleep. If he was in the zone, Lily was lightly snoring, dead to the world.

Not wanting to wake his niece, Hawes followed Helena to the seating area in the opposite corner. Helena collapsed on the couch, and Hawes started for one of the two armchairs before remembering the ice pack on his back. He grabbed the chair from the other paper-strewn desk, rolled it over, and turned it so he could straddle it, arms folded on top.

"Any blowback on the warehouse?" Hawes asked.

"We're clear," Helena said. "Local station got a tip that the cartel was cleaning up its own mess. And the feds?"

"Happy to have a new cartel informant."

"Nice save there." Amelia stepped away from the crib, shook out her long brown hair, and squeezed Holt's arm. "You can stop, babe. She's out cold."

"Just finishing this last bit of detail work on Jodie and Ray."

Hawes rotated his chair. "How'd you set that up?"

"Third party, like Perry suggested."

"How—"

Holt pointed at his wireless earbud, then at the EMS live streams running on one of his monitors. "Heard the call come in. Hacked the neighbor's security doorbell footage. I considered the fight option, but given their injuries and gunshot trajectory, there had to be a third party."

"You wipe the security footage?" Hawes asked.

"Of course." Holt gave him a what-do-you-take-me-for look that made Hawes smile. "And the footage from the ATM across the street."

"Sloppy, Big H," Helena remarked.

She wasn't wrong. He expected more of himself. While he'd cleaned up the unexpected hiccup in the warehouse, he'd made a mess of things in the alley. It seemed everything had been off-kilter since Dante Perry's arrival.

"He checks out," Holt said, as if reading his mind.

The twin-speak and mind reading were about the only "twin" things Hawes and his brother shared. Where Hawes's light-brown hair was streaked with blond, Holt's dirty-blond was tinged with red. Hawes had the same cold blue eyes as Helena, miles away from Holt's warm brown. Hawes preferred suits, Holt flannel and jeans. And where most of Hawes's physical features were lean and overly sharp—nose, chin, elbows, knees, even the tops of his ears —Holt was a mountain of curved, sloping muscles. Big round shoulders, a wide barrel chest inked with tattoos, redwood trunks for legs, and a strong jaw that led to a round, dimpled chin, even though Holt covered it with a brownish-red beard cut to make his face look more square.

Their mother used to joke that Hawes was so much slighter and pointier than Holt because his brother had taken up most of the space in her womb. Which was also why, she claimed, Hawes was born first, making him the big brother, technically. Carrying that guilt, joke or not, Holt had been Hawes's vigilant protector when they were young, never letting anyone bully him for being smaller, or gay. But by the time Holt had left for army basic training, Hawes had grown to a lanky six-foot-plus and learned to protect himself using the weapons he did have—speed, agility, and the same sharp elbows that had helped save him tonight.

Those and Dante Perry.

"He give you that card you sent me a picture of?" Holt asked.

Hawes pulled out his phone and opened the card compartment. "He intentionally left a thumb and index print on each corner."

Holt tossed a remote to Helena on the way to his other desk. He fished a fingerprint kit out of the bottom drawer and cleared a desk corner with a swipe of his tattooed right arm, sending a stack of mail flying.

Amelia rolled her eyes. "Really, babe?"

"I'll get it later." Meaning he'd restack the mail until Lily eventually puked on it and made disposal necessary. He waved Hawes over, extracted the card with a pair of forceps, and got to work with the fingerprint dust.

Hawes left him to it and reclaimed his chair, rotating back to Amelia and Helena on the couch. "What do we know?"

Helena clicked a button on the remote, and pictures of Dante filled the screens—outside the restaurant, at the bar with Kane, inside the dining room, and on the porch in the alley, gun arm raised.

Helena hummed, same as she had outside, and Amelia laughed. "Down girl."

"The name and business check out," Holt said as he continued to work under an exam lamp. "Though he's only recently back in San Francisco."

"Where's he been?" Hawes asked.

Helena clicked the remote again, and a list of addresses appeared on one of the screens. "Bounced around a lot."

Seattle was Dante's last known address. Explained the rocker vibe. Grunge just wouldn't die, no matter how many curses Hawes laid at its flannel feet. "He licensed as a PI here?"

"BSIS issued his license a few months back." Helena changed to another screen. "And he's got a CCW permit."

Concealed carry, likewise issued a few months back. Not uncommon for PIs. Or cops. Mercs didn't bother. But first Hawes circled back to something else his brother had said, and something Dante had mentioned too.

"You said 'recently back.' He's from here?"

"Yearbook picture," Holt said, then to Helena, "Next."

Helena clicked...and recoiled, an arm thrown dramatically over her face. "Warn a girl, Little H."

"Hey now!" Hawes jostled his sister's bare foot, which was dangling over her knee. "We weren't all born beauty queens."

Staring at seventeen-year-old Dante Perry, Hawes felt more than a shred of sympathy for the awkward boy Dante had been. Features too big for his face, gangly limbs, an unruly cowlick. Hawes had been there. Had the bad school pictures to prove it too. His eyes flickered to the bottom of the page. Galileo High School. Before it became Galileo Academy, it would have been the closest public high school to the heavily Italian North Beach neighborhood. Dante had said he'd grown up in San Francisco. "Family still in North Beach?" Hawes ventured.

"Mom and a sister," Holt replied, back at his computers. He snapped a picture of the dusty card with his phone, tapped the screen a few times, then, after keying in commands on the computer, stepped back and wiped his hands off on his jeans. "Okay, that's done and analyzing."

"What else did Perry say to you?" Amelia asked.

"That someone in the organization wants to kill me."

Helena scoffed. "Tell us something we don't know."

Hawes curled his fingers in the fabric of the sling stretched over his chest. "That it's somehow connected to Isabelle Costa."

Indrawn breaths echoed all around. Holt wobbled where he sat on the couch arm next to his wife, and Helena took up tapping her nails against each other.

"Does Perry have any connection to her?" Amelia asked, the first to recover. Holt and Helena still looked off-balance.

Welcome to Hawes's world. "Not that I know of." He turned to his brother. "Dig deeper. See if their paths crossed. See if anyone is paying him. Is this business or personal?"

"Looked personal to me out there," Helena said with a nod toward the front of the house. "How are *you* gonna handle him? Something tells me you'll be seeing him again soon."

Hawes didn't disagree with her read, and that prospect —of seeing Dante again, sooner rather than later—both excited and troubled him. There was no denying the pull he'd felt, or that Dante had saved his life, but there was also no denying he was a threat to Hawes's family, given what he seemed to suspect about Isabelle's death. If Dante ever learned the truth, he'd be an enemy for sure. And there were more than enough of those these days. Except this one had already provided valuable information that had helped save Hawes. There could be more to learn.

"I'm going to work a potential source," Hawes said. "See what more he can tell us about Ray and Jodie and whose orders they were following. I'll use whomever I can to find out who's gunning for us."

"For *you*," Amelia said. "That's all we know so far."

"True, but all of you should be on guard. If this is the start of a coup…"

"Then they'll have to take us all down." Helena's voice had taken on that chilly edge again, her protective hackles rising once more.

"If Perry's got information, get it," Holt said. "I've got no flags and no unusual account activity on either Ray or Jodie." Everyone in the organization was monitored for irregular financial or travel activity, as well as potential points of leverage.

"They had to know and trust the person who hired them," Helena said.

"Because they believed the payout would be there," Amelia added, finishing the same train of thought that had occurred to Hawes earlier.

He nodded. "We need to find out who."

"How much did you tell Brax?" Helena asked.

"Nothing, but I did agree to give him a heads-up if things were going"—he cleared his throat and forced out the words—"tits-up."

Holt snickered. "Once more with feeling, Big H."

Hawes shifted and yanked at the sling, jiggling the ice pack on his back. "Do you want me to throw this bag of ice at you?"

"Brax is about to throw ice on both of you," Helena announced.

Sure enough, the chief, pissed-off scowl in place, was

charging up the stairs to the front door. There was no time to stop him before he—

The doorbell chimed, and two seconds later Lily's muffled whimpers broke into a wail.

Holt bolted up, scooping his daughter out of the crib and into his arms.

"I'll go grab a bottle," Amelia said, likewise springing into parental action, their routine well practiced.

Holt installed himself in the rocker, the world forgotten as Lily, cradled like a football in his tattooed arm, became the center of his universe.

Hawes was more than fine with that. She was the reason they did any of this. They'd all give her the world if they could. Impossible, but what they could do was make it better and safer for her. Hawes leaned over and kissed the munchkin's fuzzy auburn head, then his brother's. "Get her settled. We'll handle Kane."

He waited for Helena to finish locking the computers, then followed her downstairs. She stopped abruptly on the second-floor landing, and if not for both their quick reflexes, Hawes would have run her over. "You need to change," she said, nodding to his old room, next to hers, where he still kept a closet full of clothes for when he crashed there, which happened frequently. "You've been home a while, remember?" She nudged the ice pack on his back. "And there's a wet spot here."

"You got Kane?"

"Yeah, I got him," she said with a wink.

He started toward his room, feeling more than a little sorry for the chief. He barely made it a step before Helena grasped his wrist and turned him back around. "Are you okay?"

Cattiness gone, she wore the same concerned expression she had when Hawes had uttered Isabelle's name. She'd been there that night. She'd had to drag him out of the shower when, no matter how hard he scrubbed, he couldn't seem to get the blood off his hands.

He couldn't lie to her now. "No, but I have to be."

FIVE

It was half past two by the time the Lyft pulled to the curb in front of Hawes's building. As predicted, Kane had read them the riot act, then questioned them in-depth about Jodie and Ray. Holt's cover story had held and was supported by the evidence called in. Relatively satisfied, or just dog-tired, Kane had given them a much sterner warning to keep him apprised of any situations, then cleared out. Hawes had done the same shortly thereafter, against Helena's wishes. She'd wanted him to stay at the house, but Hawes needed to decompress within the comfort of his own four walls.

Holt had swept the area around the four-story South Beach condo building and confirmed all was clear. Inside the unit was always a risk—Hawes refused interior cameras—but exterior footage from the past few hours showed only the usual residents entering the building. No one approached his end-unit's door.

Apparently they hadn't looked hard enough, or more likely, the man leaning against the side of the building reading a paperback, knew exactly where to stand to avoid the cameras.

"Where's the bike?" Hawes asked. All the building's parking areas were in view of Holt's or other surrounding cameras. They would have seen the Hog on the security footage.

"In a garage up the block," Dante answered as he tucked away the book, a popular fantasy series. "One that doesn't have wired cameras."

Caution dictated—more and more with each passing hour—that Hawes not let this man into his life, much less into his home. A well-founded warning. A perfectly timed kill. A work-around designed to thwart their security. Letting him in was a risk, but Hawes had committed to keeping this potential enemy close, to seeing what more he knew about the threat to his family, should he make another approach. And now here he was.

Those were the logical reasons to let Dante in. There was also the illogical. The part of Hawes that had been unsteady since the alley, that he'd kept hidden from his siblings, and that was already settling in Dante's presence. When Dante shoved off the wall and stepped directly into a camera's line of sight, it settled further.

"Could have given you a ride if you'd wanted." The smirk was for Hawes's benefit. The dark eyes flitting to the camera were for the benefit of whoever was watching. A white flag of sorts. He was exposing himself here as much as Hawes.

Good enough for Hawes, whose traitorous body led his mind astray, considering other things he'd like to ride. He pushed back one side of his leather jacket and dug his keys out of his jeans pocket, ignoring his vibrating phone in the other. "If I never ride on that bike again, it'll be too soon." He swiped his key fob over the building's lock and opened the front door for Dante to enter ahead of him. Less risk, relatively.

"You need to be more careful," Dante said, as if reading his mind.

"Right now, I trust about five people." Keeping Dante in front of him, Hawes motioned for the stairwell. "None of whom were in a position to drive me home. A Lyft tracks where I'm picked up, where I'm dropped off, and when my card is charged. Holt can track all that. And the person in my organization who wants to kill me isn't going to kill a civilian who's just trying to make a living."

Dante exited on the second floor without being told. Worry shifted forward in Hawes's mind—the PI knew exactly where he lived—until Dante's next words took the lead. "You sure about that?"

"I have to be," Hawes said, "if I'm going to sleep at night."

He wouldn't have another Isabelle Costa weighing on his conscience. Though maybe others didn't have the same moral hang-ups he did. Was that why someone was targeting him? Were their associates opposed to the new order? Five years in, it wasn't so new anymore, and no income had been lost, no innocents had been killed, and no one had gone to jail. Hawes counted those things as victories, but perhaps other operatives didn't. Operatives like Jodie and Ray who'd been frustrated with Hawes at different points tonight. Longer than that, apparently.

"Madigan?" Dante called from the far end of the hallway.

Hawes shook himself loose from where he'd halted

midstep. At the door, he pressed his thumb to the scanner and entered his access code, the security significantly upgraded on his unit. "Sorry," he said to Dante. "Was just replaying the follow-up with Kane." A convenient enough excuse.

"He came by the house?"

"To discuss what looked like a third-party altercation." Inside, Hawes tapped the foyer light switch, and track lighting brightened the hallway leading into the condo's main living area. He toed off his shoes and shrugged out of his jacket, tossing both on the steps to the master bedroom loft. "Holt thanks you for that suggestion. Quicker back-story build."

A shadow streaked across the edge of the lighted area.

Dante drew his gun and lunged forward, a hand on Hawes's chest to hold him back. Considering for a split-second how much it would hurt his aching back and hands, Hawes acted anyway. Bandaged hands wrapped around Dante's wrist, he wrenched the hand away and crouched. He turned under Dante's outstretched arm and kicked, heel aimed at Dante's firing wrist. Direct hit. The gun clattered to the floor. With Dante's other wrist still in his hands, Hawes righted himself, spun behind Dante, yanked the man's arm up behind his back, and rammed him, chest first, into the wooden pillar by the stairs.

Dante struggled against the hold, but Hawes kept him pinned, arm twisted between them, leg thrust between Dante's thighs, his knee pressed to the pole.

"Why are you attacking me?" Dante gritted out, voice low.

Hawes, fearing no danger, didn't bother to moderate his volume. "Because I don't want you to shoot my cat."

The tense body under his relaxed and shook with laughter.

Hawes took a half step back, whipped Dante around to face him, and hand to his chest, shoved him back against the pole. "And because you need to know I can take care of myself. Don't ever do that again."

Dante lifted his hands, palms out. "Understood," he said with a smile. It faded, however, as he reached out and used his thumb to catch a bead of sweat trickling down the side of Hawes's face. "Fit guy like you breaks a sweat from a few self-defense moves?"

Hawes wanted to chase after the touch—rough and gentle, warm and dangerous—but he stepped away instead, using the opposite wall for support. "Ray brought his pistol down on my back before you got there."

"Must've been the shout I heard." Dante retrieved his gun, tucked it into his waistband, and crossed the hall in two strides. "And I saw what you did to your other associate. I know you can take care of yourself."

Hawes rested his head against the wall, trying to put space between them where there wasn't any. Dante had more muscle on his frame, but at about the same height, they were practically nose-to-nose. "Then what are you doing here?"

"You owe me a thank-you."

Laughter bubbled out of Hawes, unexpected and welcome, even if it did set off another ripple of back spasms. He grasped Dante's biceps, rotated him toward the main area, and gave him a shove. "I wasn't sure if that rock-star strut was an act or if you were that damn arrogant."

Dante grinned over his shoulder. "I've been called worse."

"I'm sure."

At the end of the hall, Hawes hit the next set of switches, illuminating the open-plan kitchen, den, and dining areas. Track lighting hanging from the overhead beams reflected off polished hardwood floors, white cabinets and counter-tops, sterling-gray walls, and huge windows and glass balcony doors in the brick wall at the far end of the space.

Dante circled the den, laying his jacket and gun on the leather couch, while Hawes scratched behind the ears of his black Bombay cat, who'd taken up position on the dining table. She clawed at the bandages on his hand and hissed at the stranger in their domain. "Iris doesn't like you."

"Iris doesn't know me." Nevertheless, Dante wisely steered clear of her claws and came to a stop next to the rolling wooden ladder, which was locked in place on its short track. "Nice place, though I'm not sure about the ladder to nowhere." He snaked an arm through the rungs, showing off his broad chest and flexing biceps.

Hawes licked his lips. *Even better than the abs.*

"You want to show me?" Dante said.

"I hardly know you," he hedged. "You're lucky I let you in at all."

"Doesn't stop you from picking up guys in the clubs when you go out."

He'd been tracking him, then. Hawes tucked away that piece of information. "Those guys don't open by telling me someone wants to kill me."

"I may have gone about that wrong," Dante conceded.

"If you were trying to get into my pants, yes."

"Into your head?"

Mission accomplished there. Hawes ignored the phone buzzing in his pocket and rested a hip on the corner of the built-in desk behind the couch. As much distance as he could get from the too tempting man leaning against the ladder. "What do you want, Mr. Perry?"

"I want to stop the person trying to unseat you."

"My guardian angel sent from North Beach." Hawes folded his arms. "And why is that?"

Dante's posture remained casual, but his gaze sharpened, dark and ominous. "Because I think the same person is responsible for Isabelle Costa's death."

"Her death was ruled a domestic disturbance. Her boyfriend also died at the scene."

"We both know that's a load of horseshit."

Hawes remained motionless, even as bile stung the back of his throat. "Who was she to you?" he asked, trying to crack that door open wider.

"Someone who mattered."

She'd mattered to Hawes too. Not enough before her death, the world after.

He fled the scene of the crime a second time, avoiding Dante's gaze and ambling in the direction of the glass and brick wall. Ignoring the pair of tufted leather accent chairs, he draped his arms over the diagonal seismic strut, staring out the balcony windows and watching the fog creep into the moonlit courtyard. "I meant what I said at Danko. I always expect someone wants to kill me."

"Did you expect your lieutenants to make an actual attempt?"

No, the threats had never been so direct—so close. Two of his most loyal operatives turning on him right after they'd successfully pulled off another job together. No flags, no warnings. If Dante hadn't been there, would Hawes have ducked in time to avoid Ray's shot? Would he be lying dead in that alley too? Would the rest of his family be far behind? Hawes closed his eyes and fought against the cold shiver that had slithered around his ankles all night, that snaked through him now like the fog outside.

Heat hit his back, and big, strong hands settled on his hips. "Let me help you."

Hawes leaned into the warmth, letting it chase away the chill, steadying him from the points of contact inward. "I hardly know you," he repeated, much less hedging, much more wanting. Need eclipsing caution.

Dante nuzzled behind his ear, nose and lips teasing the sensitive hollow there. "We could change that."

Hawes reveled in the offered heat and in the faint whiff of eucalyptus that wafted under his nose, the ends of Dante's hair tickling his shoulders. He opened his eyes, and their reflection in the window—broad, dark, and handsome framing his leaner, pale form—almost did Hawes in.

"Liked that suit tonight," Dante said. "Like this jeans-and-tank look better." He grasped the hem of Hawes's white tank and curled it in his fist, inching the fabric up and exposing skin.

Hawes watched, on the knife's edge of anticipation, gut clenched with desire, as Dante's other hand skated off his hip and slid toward his bared abs. He arched his back, wanting to feel Dante's touch on his skin, wanting to thrust his ass back to feel if other parts of Dante were as hard as his.

Reality had other ideas, and a spike of pain arced up Hawes's spine. "Fuck," he cursed, eyes scrunching closed as he leaned forward, fingers curling around the edge of the metal strut.

Dante's hand flattened over his back, gently rubbing. "You take anything for the pain?"

He shook his head. Amelia had offered, but he'd refused, wanting to stay clearheaded.

"You got ibuprofen around here?"

"Top drawer of the desk."

The heat at his back disappeared, and Hawes suppressed a whimper of disappointment. He slouched against another of the wooden support poles and tracked Dante around the condo, watching as the PI collected the bottle of pills and a glass of water. He brought them to Hawes, who tipped out two pills and tossed them back with a gulp of water. "Thanks."

"I saw what you did in that alley," Dante said as he took the glass and bottle from Hawes and set them aside. "Impressive."

"I have to be."

Dante braced his forearm on the pole over Hawes's head and crowded his side. "You don't have to do it alone."

He wasn't alone. He had his family and his trusted inner circle…as soon as he figured out who among them he could still trust. Beyond that? Maybe one day he'd have what Holt did with Amelia. What his parents and grandparents had enjoyed. A partner who got it, who understood and accepted what he did and stood by his side. Who'd help him protect his family and the empire they'd built. Fuck, he wanted that, but until then, he could only depend on himself and his family. Not on a stranger whose aims would ultimately be at cross-purposes with his. No matter how tempting the offered comfort was in the present moment.

His phone buzzed in his pocket again, right on cue.

"That's my brother or sister," he said. "They saw us enter the building and condo together. If I don't answer soon, they're going to think you killed me."

Dante slipped a hand into Hawes's pocket, fingertips so close to where Hawes wanted them. The asshole grinned as he slowly removed the vibrating device and gently laid it in Hawes's bandaged palm. "Tell them you're set for a guard tonight." He loped over to the couch and picked up his coat, digging out his book. He tossed the coat onto the coffee table, shoved his gun under the couch pillow, and stretched out, one hand holding the book, the other tucked behind his head, those fucking biceps flexed to top temptation.

"How do I trust you won't kill me in my sleep?" Hawes sniped, more out of sexual frustration than any real fear. He felt more like himself than he had all night. Steady again.

"Same way I'm going to have to trust you not to kill me. You are the Prince of Killers, aren't you?"

Hawes bit his tongue, fighting the words that wanted to form. Twice in one night. Hawes's hate for the title crested once more. Hate that he was the prince when it was actually the three of them—him, Holt, and Helena—running the organization. Hate that he'd been forced into the role because he was the oldest, technically, and hate that when someone had to make the tough decisions, it was always him. He'd been the prince since he was sixteen and had given the doctors permission to turn off his parents' ventilators when neither his grandparents, who were absent at the time, nor his siblings could make the call.

Cold as ice, the stories went.

He hated the killer part just as much. It implied malice, evilness, and cruelty when Hawes had strived to take those variables out of the equation. He knew what he was, what his family did, but there was a place for them, a need for assassins in a world where people didn't play by the rules and legal justice missed its mark. He'd felt like a killer only twice in his life—that morning in the hospital when he'd become the prince, and that night three years ago when he'd spilled an innocent woman's blood. A day that had somehow brought into his life the man now stretched out on his couch. And Hawes needed him to think he was the Prince of Killers, for both their sakes.

For now.

So he held his words, bottled his hate, and exerted control over his body, his emotions, and the situation. He ignored the part of himself that desperately wanted to let go and accept Dante's offer to get to know him better. Ignored the twin flares of pain as he flexed his hands and straightened his spine. Ignored the bitterness in his mouth and in his soul as he declared, "I am," before retreating to his bedroom, alone.

SIX

Sprawled on his back, Hawes stared at the ceiling of his lofted bedroom, counting the rings around a knot in one of the wooden planks. From there he counted the planks and beams themselves, the track lighting fixtures, the sprinkler heads on the exposed pipes, and the cables that ran along the beam directly over his head and down the pillars on either side of the bed. The numbers hadn't changed since he'd counted an hour ago, when the gray light of morning had first trickled over the loft's half wall. Hadn't changed since yesterday morning, or since the morning after he'd bought the place once he'd turned thirty and could access his trust fund.

The counting usually helped after he woke from a nightmare, but only if it was light out. The predawn darkness was hell. Without light, all he could do was count the mistakes he'd made that night three years ago, replaying them over and over. Not fully vetting the tip. Giving chase without backup. Assuming the other passenger in the van was a traitor too, one who'd kill him or blow the van, exposing his family either way. Squeezing the trigger before he made a positive ID. Spending the first few hours of his thirtieth birthday scrubbing blood from his hands. There was more to the count, but those were the low points. They replayed in his head until it was light enough to count other things, to force himself back to sleep for a few hours. Today, however, those stolen hours of early morning sleep were out of reach, the smell of coffee and the sound of voices drifting up from the kitchen below.

His siblings had let themselves in fifteen minutes ago, set the coffee to brew, and Helena had commenced the grilling. "You don't have a bed of your own?" was her latest pointed inquiry. A little too pointed, the wrong direction, in Hawes's opinion.

"Hena!" he shouted, making his wakefulness known. "Leave him be."

"I have a sister," Dante called back. "I get it."

Hawes didn't think he did, unless Dante's sister was an attorney too. He needed to get down there. He tested his hands first—some lingering soreness, but under the bandages, his palms were back to normal. He threw off the quilted comforter and moved quickly but deliberately, careful not to antagonize his stiff back that wasn't as well recovered as his hands. He shooed Iris off last night's jeans, pulled them on with a clean T-shirt, and shoved his feet into a pair of flip-flops.

Helena, meanwhile, continued her cross-examination. "Where's your sister?"

"Here in the city," Dante answered.

"Your family?"

"Also here."

She was testing him and the answers she already had. "How long have you been a PI?"

"Going on ten years."

"Before that?"

Dante rattled off addresses and post-college odd jobs, all of which had been covered by Holt's background check. Relatively reassured himself, Hawes took the stairs down and ducked into the bathroom, brushed his teeth, popped a few ibuprofen, pitched the bandages, and washed up, then joined the others.

"Excuse her," he said. "She can't turn the lawyer off."

"Is that it?" Dante eyed the steak knife Helena was using to spread cream cheese on a toasted bagel.

"Just getting to know your new bodyguard," she quipped.

"Is that it?" Hawes parroted. He strolled past them and over to the couch where Holt sat, a laptop open on his knees, Lily in a polka-dot sling against his chest. Hawes brushed the baby's auburn fuzz, and his niece stared up at him with big brown eyes that were going to cause them all a truckload of grief one day. For now, she was quiet, content to be nestled against her father's chest. "Amelia on shift?"

"Seven to seven," Holt answered without missing a keystroke, his focus on whatever search he was running.

Hawes let him be and returned to the kitchen, claiming one of the metal barstools at the island. "Status?"

Helena handed him a coffee and cut her eyes to their visitor.

"He's not going anywhere. Not without answering some questions."

She gasped in mock offense. "You just told me to go easy."

"Not what I said." Hawes wrapped his hands around the mug, savoring its warmth, and took a long swallow. He curled forward, stretching out his back, then straightened slowly, flexing the other direction. The stiffness eased, and Hawes sighed in relief. He took another sip and returned his gaze to Helena. "You weren't asking the questions I want answers to." He shifted his attention to Dante. "What led you to the restaurant last night? To me?"

"Got a tip about a shift inside your organization. One that may not be to everyone's liking."

"From who?"

"Don't know."

Helena crunched through her bagel, loudly. Hawes would have laughed if not for his own mounting frustration. "That's not particularly helpful."

"You may have accelerated matters," Helena said around her bite.

Dante leaned against the stainless-steel fridge, mug in hand. "Or flushed the traitors out into the open so you're aware of the problem and can deal with it."

"Speaking of…" Hawes rotated toward Holt. "Did you find anything else on Jodie and Ray?"

"As far as deposits, no."

Hawes didn't need twin-speak to discern the caveat in Holt's answer. "But withdrawals?"

"They made an unscheduled stop on the way back from Paso Robles last week."

"Shit," Dante murmured. "The hit on the winemaker was your group, and last night's warehouse fire was part two of the job. It wasn't the cartel doing cleanup. It was you."

"I remember Jodie and Ray being delayed," Helena said,

skipping right over Dante's remark. It was one thing to acknowledge Dante's awareness of the organization. It was another to admit to the exact details of a hit. "They were a day late getting back. Said they were waylaid by car trouble so we didn't flag it."

"At a remote coastal inn?" Holt nodded at his computer screen.

Hawes stepped behind him and peered at the hotel website on-screen. He whistled low. "Were they taking the scenic route?"

"If they were, Avery and Lucas were taking it too, off-book." Holt popped up two more windows, each displaying credit card account registers with similar charges for the same night. "There weren't any other operatives there," he added, answering Hawes's next question. "Just these four."

At least there was that, but still, two more high-ranking, trusted associates were possibly involved. "It had to be someone Jodie and Ray trusted," he said, echoing their conclusion from last night.

"Avery and Lucas would fit," his sister replied.

"Shit!" He pushed off the back of the couch and locked his hands behind his head, ignoring the ache in his back as he paced in front of the windows. Avery and Lucas weren't just high-level turncoats. They were also the two people who'd accompanied Helena to the scene of Isabelle's death. Who'd found Hawes on his knees on the rain-slicked asphalt, trying to staunch the flow of blood from a gunshot wound he'd delivered. He was starting to think Dante was right. Whatever was happening now was connected to what had happened then, on the night Isabelle Costa died.

That fact acknowledged—and the anxiety and unease

that came with it internalized—a calm settled over Hawes. He counted the panes in the windows, waited for his breath and heartbeat to slow, then dropped his arms and turned back to his condo full of visitors. "I'll see what I can find out today at the pier."

"I've got a hearing at ten." Helena dumped her empty paper plate into the trash. "If I don't go by the station beforehand, I'll swing by there after. I can be at HQ by one."

"No," Hawes said. "Things need to appear as usual. I would normally be in this morning. You wouldn't."

"I'll go in with you," Holt said. He patted Lily's back through the sling. "She's having fun being out today."

Dante pushed off the fridge. "And I'll have their backs."

Helena blocked his forward momentum with her arm. "Look here, Mr. Hair—"

"Hena," Hawes chided, while Holt laughed.

Their sister, however, held the steak knife at-the-ready and had drawn nose-to-chest with Dante, though you wouldn't know it by her stance. For all she cared, she was taller than Dante, not a good foot shorter. "You've gotta give us more before I let you walk into this with my family."

"There's a flash drive in my coat pocket."

"I've got it," Hawes said, saving Holt the trouble of reaching around the baby and laptop. He retrieved the flash drive—generic, drugstore model—and held it out to Holt.

Holt's wary gaze split between him and Dante. "I'm not putting that in my computer without checking it for viruses."

"I wouldn't either," Dante said. "Which was why I checked it before I put it in mine. No viruses, I swear."

Holt still hesitated. Hawes slapped the drive into his

hand with a firm, "Just do it." They didn't have time to argue.

Hawes moved behind Holt so he could view the screen as Holt disconnected from servers and wireless networks before inserting the flash drive. No blue screen of death appeared. Holt released a held breath, and Hawes put a hand on his shoulder, squeezing gently. Then harder, unintentionally, when Holt opened the first unnamed folder and the screen filled with surveillance photos—of Hawes. From various spots around town, from the pier, from outside the family fort in Pac Heights, and in front of his condo. Each had a bull's-eye drawn on his head.

Hawes rotated toward Dante, who perched on a barstool. "You could have taken these. Manipulated them."

"He didn't," Holt said before Dante could answer. "This footage was taken, edited, and loaded from an MCS computer." Hawes trusted his interpretation of the terminal window full of code gibberish.

"Can you find out who?" Helena asked.

"It'll take time, but yeah. Should be able to."

Was this someone making a grab for power or someone helping them stay in power? Hawes bet the former, given the bull's-eye, but why had they sent this to Dante? "Is this the tip you were talking about?"

"Open the other folder," he said, noticeably grimmer.

Holt double-clicked on the icon, and Hawes's nightmares sprang to life in pixelated form. Pictures of Isabelle's crime scene splashed across the screen.

"Your organization shifted that night," Dante said.

It had. No indiscriminate killing, no collateral damage, no unvetted targets. Hawes's rules—for himself and the organization. And he was working to get them out of the explosives business. The warehouse job was intended to be the last time they used them. All because of what happened that night three years ago.

Heavy footsteps to Hawes's right indicated Dante's approach. Hawes shot him a pointed glare, and he halted next to the closest pillar, leaning a shoulder there. "I'm a PI," he said. "It's not hard to follow the breadcrumbs. Someone doesn't like the shift."

"And you care because?"

"Less death is a good thing."

Helena chuckled darkly. "You do realize who you're talking to, right?"

"Less innocent death." Dante straightened, long legs spread shoulder-width apart, bulging arms folded over his chest. He cut an imposing figure. "I want to know what happened to Isabelle that night. The truth, not the bullshit cover story. And I think this is the way in."

"You're using us," Hawes said.

"I am." There wasn't an ounce of shame in his admission. Cocky, arrogant, sexy. Honest. "It's in my interest to keep you all alive."

Until he got his answers. Once he learned the truth, where would his interests lie then? Hawes didn't think it would be with keeping them alive.

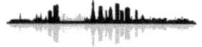

In the back seat of Holt's SUV, his pinky finger clutched in his niece's tiny fist, Hawes watched as Dante, in front of him, struggled to take in all the new development around them. "You might be from San Francisco, but you haven't been down here in a while, have you?" Hawes said.

"I've driven by it on the freeway and seen it on sat-photos, but seeing it for real..." He dropped his book into his lap. "Christ, it's like a different place around here."

He wasn't wrong. The Central Waterfront/Dogpatch neighborhood, just south of the Giants ballpark, the UCSF Medical Center, and the Warriors arena, had been radically redeveloped over the past two decades. Around the ship-yards and piers that used to dominate the area, office build-ings, research labs, and apartments had sprung up, along with restaurants, coffee shops, and other retailers to support the neighborhood's new residents and visitors.

"Last time I was through here," Dante said, head swivel-ing, "it was parking lots for the ballpark and run-down piers."

Not surprising. Even if Dante hadn't been away until recently, in a place like San Francisco, one could go years without stepping foot in different parts of the city; its many neighborhoods separated as they were by topography, traf-fic, cultures, even the weather. Hell, it'd been more than a decade since Hawes had ventured into Golden Gate Park. He suspected the little girl holding his finger would change that soon enough.

Holt steered the SUV off Third, onto the road to the pier, and a couple of minutes later, eased the SUV to a stop in front of Madigan Cold Storage's retractable metal gate.

Hawes rolled down the rear window. "The piers and warehouses have come a long way too." He flipped open the nondescript box beside the intercom and thumbed the scanner. The touchpad turned green, and the gate began to swing open.

"High security," Dante said.

"Have you met my baby brother?"

Holt held up two fingers as he drove through. "By two minutes."

Hawes clapped his biceps. "And don't you forget it, Little H."

Two fingers became Holt's single middle one, and a sexy laugh rumbled out of Dante. The first of the day, and it made Hawes smile. Until he stepped out of the car and the easy mood evaporated. Suspecting your employees' occasional murderous intent and actually experiencing it were two very different things.

Holt nudged him out of the way and reached in to eject Lily's car seat.

Lily...here, where maybe there was someone trying to kill Hawes. Fuck, what were they thinking? "Holt, maybe you should—"

"No, we talked about this. We follow the regular routine." He handed Lily's carrier to Hawes, shouldered her diaper bag, and shut the door. "Besides, we have Mr. Hair for backup."

Dante rolled his eyes. "That nickname's gonna stick, isn't it?"

"They still call me Little H, and I'm bigger than both of them combined." Holt took Lily's car seat from Hawes and headed toward the main entrance. His gait defined military precision, even weighed down by the baby and her gear.

"You want to show me this fancy building of yours?" Dante said at Hawes's side.

Dante's easy manner, taken together with Holt's nonchalance, reminded Hawes that yes, while there were potential threats, they were more than equipped to handle them. Hawes ran a hand through his damp hair, fluffing the long top strands to cover his damnable cowlick, and buttoned the suit coat he'd changed into after a quick shower at the condo. "Yes, let me show you around." And let whoever might be targeting him see he wasn't afraid and that there was a new player on the board.

Rather than following Holt to the main entrance at the center of the three-story, U-shaped building, Hawes led Dante through the south wing first, where cold storage units stored products for fisheries and food service companies. Midmorning, this side of the building was mostly deserted, just a few employees double-checking freezer settings. By contrast, the north wing, where cold storage units were manufactured for use by MCS and for sale to customers, was noisy and bustling—engineers checking plans, factory technicians operating assembly lines, quality control professionals approving finished components.

"Quite the contrast," Dante said as Hawes led him toward the office portion in the middle of the building.

"Most suppliers and customers have come and gone already. Third-shift employees guide them through the early morning rush. Though at least half of the workers tend to linger in the main building after shift."

Today was no different. The ground-floor cafeteria and lounge areas were busy, third-shift employees grabbing food and waiting for the rush hour traffic to die down. The second floor looked and sounded like any other office— printers, copiers, keystrokes. All of MCS's admin for order-ing, receiving, and processing happened here. It was also the company's gossip hub, which was working overtime today, the whispering growing louder as Hawes passed through with Dante.

"Guessing you're the topic of the day," Hawes said as he

pressed a thumb to the stairwell keypad. The lock clicked, and Hawes pushed the door open.

Dante waited until he closed the door to run a hand down the sleeve of Hawes's navy suit coat. "This one's even nicer, and more fitted, than the gray one yesterday." He plucked at the cuff of the light-blue shirt sleeve peeking out from the jacket, then started up the steps. "You wear suits like this to work all the time?"

"I do," Hawes said, his gruff voice echoing in the stairwell.

Dante grinned back at him. "Those whispers aren't about me."

Hawes begged to differ, but the third-floor door swung open before he got the chance.

"Saw you coming." Holt stood in the doorway, his massive bulk blocking the entrance. His brown eyes glanced at Dante, then flitted over the PI's shoulder to lock with Hawes's.

Hawes knew what his brother was thinking, the silent question he was asking. How far do we let him in? Hawes had had the same argument with himself on the ride over. While they'd gotten a bit more out of the PI at the condo, Hawes still had a mountain of questions. At the same time, he sensed he was going to have to give some to get some. Dante had been clear; he was using them too. And what was Dante going to see here that others hadn't? MCS's company conference room and executive offices? Typically on the top floor. Holt's surveillance wall? Not that uncommon for a manufacturing operation like theirs. More importantly, if there were traitors still among their operatives, *this* was the floor they would be on. Hawes wanted the extra firepower at his family's back.

He gave Holt a nod, and his brother stepped aside, allowing Dante entry. Hawes followed him onto the third floor and secured the door behind them. It wasn't nearly as loud or crowded up here.

Zoe smiled politely as they passed the conference room and main reception desk, which if anyone looked closely, was in fact a sophisticated surveillance setup. Zoe's primary objective was to warn them in the event of a breach. Her secondary objective was to hold off any intruders long enough for the floor to power down and assume the roles the rest of the company and world thought they played. Executives, support staff, and IT. Translation: Madigans, assassins, and hackers.

At the far end of the floor, overlooking the south inlet, Helena had one corner office, Hawes the other, and between them, Holt had knocked out a wall to make a single giant space for his setup, a mirror of the one at the house, except that the crib here was a pop-up version that slid under the desk when Lily wasn't with him.

Dante whistled low. "Between this"—he waved at the wall of electronics—"and the office, manufacturing, and storage functions downstairs, there's no way the original building supports the electrical load or the density of people and activity."

Hawes tossed his suit coat onto a chair. "Not in your research?"

"I can only dig so far," Dante replied. "The property is held in a family trust, so it's not regularly reassessed. There were permits pulled after Loma Prieta, and periodically since for routine upgrades and repairs, but without a change of ownership, you haven't been dinged enough for me to get a full picture."

"We saved and reinforced the foundations where we could. Along with other touches of the original structure." Hawes ran his fingers over the crenellations around the door. "Papa Cal has a thing for restoration."

"The house in Pac Heights?"

"He did all the preservation work on it." Hawes moved his hand from the fluted plaster to the steel bar that ran diagonally up to the roof. "Everything else here is seismically retrofitted and otherwise up to code, even if we don't have to be. Safer for everyone under our roof."

Dante cocked a brow.

Hawes raised one to match. "This *is* an actual business."

"With a personnel problem," Dante said.

And tour over. Back to reality, Hawes turned to Holt, who was at his keyboards. "Where are Avery and Lucas?"

A flurry of keystrokes, and then one of the monitors clicked over, showing the two operatives outside a south-wing loading dock. "Looks like they're helping with an off-load." Holt zoomed out. A cruiser was moored at the slip nearest the dock where Avery and Lucas were standing.

"We were just there," Dante said. "I didn't see them."

Neither had Hawes. "What the hell is off-loading this time of morning?"

Holt opened the day's manifests on another screen. "Nothing. Last transaction was scheduled for and clocked at seven."

"Looks to me like they're on-boarding," Dante said.

Hawes peered at the screen, and sure enough, Avery was carrying a box *from* the dock to Lucas, who ferried it onto the boat and below deck. "Keep it monitored," he said to Holt, then to Dante, "Ready to provide that backup you promised?"

Dark eyes glittered dangerously. "I'm all yours."

"Wait!" Holt said, and Hawes spun back around. "We've got bigger problems." His brother pointed at the top screen, which was feeding them visual from the security cameras at the entry gate.

Kane was leaning out the window of a nondescript sedan, requesting entry. Two police cars idled behind him. This could not be good.

SEVEN

The chief stepped out of the elevator, four officers behind him. Holt tensed in his chair on one side of Hawes, while Dante leaned against the conference room window behind them. He had their backs, but he was staying out of this. Hawes stood as Kane left his officers in the lobby and stalked across the reception area, unimpeded. Zoe was elsewhere on the floor, doing her job. Hawes was confident the three of them could deal with Kane quickly, before they lost Avery and Lucas to either their escape or law enforcement.

Kane pushed open the glass door, practically growling. "You didn't show up at the station this morning."

"Helena was supposed to stop by on her way to the courthouse."

"Your sister was not the one with Jodie and Ray before their deaths."

"*Hours* before," Hawes replied. "We went over all this last night."

Kane withdrew a folded piece of paper from inside his jacket pocket and slid it across the table. "In connection with the investigation of their murders, we have a warrant to search the premises."

"I thought that was a dispute between them and a third party," Hawes said. "What's it got to do with us?"

"They worked here, didn't they?" Kane gave a subtle nod to the warrant, and Holt reached for it. He unfolded the paper where Hawes could see, including the hand-written note from Helena inside.

Let them search. Limited parameters.

Kane was just doing his job, and Helena had already cleared it. The other clearance Hawes was waiting for appeared a moment later, Zoe back at the reception desk. "Go ahead," he said to Kane. "Zoe will show your officers to Jodie's and Ray's workspaces."

"They won't find anything," Holt said, once Kane stepped out. "This is why it pays to be paperless."

"Nothing's on paper?" Dante asked behind them.

"Not if we can help it," Hawes said.

Kane reentered the room, but before any of them could speak, a high-pitched wail erupted from the crib they'd rolled into the corner. Holt pushed up from the table. "It's like she knows you're here," he muttered.

Kane's foul mood broke on a genuine smile. "I can't help that she likes me."

"Oh, is that what you think it is?" Holt lifted the baby out of the crib, and Kane walked over close enough to coo without appearing too interested to anyone outside the conference room's glass walls.

As much as the sight warmed Hawes's heart, he needed to move this along. "Do you need me for anything else?" he asked Kane.

The chief shoved his hands in his pockets. "Any new developments?"

"We're looking into it."

"Dammit, Hawes."

"It's under control."

"I wouldn't count on it," Dante said, Holt's tablet in hand. "They're picking up the pace." He handed Hawes the tablet, open on the surveillance feed of the south-side loading bays. Avery and Lucas were hustling, as if they were using the police presence as a distraction. Or trying to move something out before the police found it.

"Do you need me for anything else?" Hawes repeated his question.

"Go handle it," Kane said. "We'll catch up later."

Hawes slipped out of the conference room, Dante on his heels. They took the stairwell to the ground floor and exited out the back of the building. At the south corner, Hawes halted, back against the wall. "With the cops on-site, let's get them on the boat."

"Close quarters," Dante said, "if a fight breaks out."

"I'm fine with that." The ibuprofen he'd taken that morning had done its work, dulling most of the lingering pain in his back and hands. "You?"

"Not a problem for me."

"Figured not."

Dante moved to draw his gun, and Hawes clasped his forearm. "Not unless you have to. We have an inkling they might not be loyal, but that suspicion hasn't been fully vetted. We need to question them first. Let's be sure, or as sure as we can be."

Something like surprise dashed across Dante's eyes. Surely he wasn't caught off-guard by Hawes's caution, not if he knew as much about the changes Hawes had made as he'd implied.

In any event, Dante got on board, leaving his gun in his waistband. "Who are you going to say I am, if they ask?"

"I'll tell them you're not a cop, *if* they ask. Otherwise, it's not their job to make personnel decisions or to question mine."

Dante's grin returned. "There he is."

Hawes agreed, the undertaking making him feel more like himself again. He rolled up his shirt sleeves. "Let's do this."

They rounded the corner, and Avery caught sight of them a few docks away. "Hey, boss," she said as they approached. Her dark eyes skittered past him to Dante, and Hawes took a step to block her view. Her attention snapped back to him, but her posture remained casual. Good call, as she couldn't be sure if Dante was friend or foe. Best not to lead on either way. "Something I can help you with? We're in a bit of a hurry here."

"Why's that?"

Her eyes flickered to Dante and back again. "Unexpected visitors."

"I'm not one," Dante said. "What are you hustling out of here?"

"Just some prototypes, to our facility in South San Francisco."

Hawes seethed. "Why the fuck are they here?"

Prototypes—a.k.a. explosives, when there were unreliable ears around—were expressly not permitted on these premises.

"Jodie and Ray delivered them yesterday," Avery said, dropping the casual act as she began to realize something was amiss. Genuine confusion colored her expression. Not fear at being caught, just fear of having pissed off the boss. "Lucas said we needed to move them ASAP."

That much was true. "Are they all loaded onto the boat?"

"Lucas is putting the last crate in the cabin now."

Hawes held an arm out toward the cruiser. "Time to go, then."

Avery boarded the stern deck first and adjusted the foldout seat into its upright position, no longer needing it as a makeshift conveyor. Hawes and Dante stepped onto the deck of the sleek cruiser, which looked like a hundred other yachts on the Bay. Fast and good cover, whether they were rescuing trafficking victims or moving illegal explosives.

"She doesn't know what's going on," Dante whispered.

Hawes agreed. "Lucas is the target."

No sooner had he said his name, than Lucas popped out from below deck, wiping his hands off on his jeans. "Avery, what's the holdup?" He straightened and locked eyes with Hawes. *Could go either way*, Hawes thought. Then Lucas caught sight of Dante, and his eyes widened with recognition. He must've gotten a report from his co-conspirators last night, before Hawes had dispatched them. His right arm went for the gun under his windbreaker.

Dante drew faster. "Wouldn't do that if I were you." He shifted to stand next to Hawes, blocking any hope Lucas had of escape.

"What the hell is going on?" Avery said from where she stood behind the steering column to Lucas's left.

His eyes flicked her direction.

Hostage.

Lucas registered the option a second later, his blue eyes flaring at the perceived advantage. He inhaled sharply, preparing to take it.

Stupid, stupid man.

Lucas dove for Avery, and Dante swung his gun, following the action. Hawes stepped in front of Dante with a sharp, "Hold!"

"Dammit, Madigan, move!"

One beat, two beats, then Hawes stepped aside…and barely held in a laugh at Dante's muttered, "Holy shit."

"She had it under control," Hawes said, eyeing Lucas's gun in Avery's hand. At her feet, Lucas lay unconscious, his arm clearly broken. If she hadn't just proven her loyalty without question, Hawes would be more than a little frightened.

"Does someone want to tell me what the fuck is going on?" she demanded.

"That's what I'm trying to figure out," Hawes said. "Steer us out of here, and you can help me."

"We're docked, boss," Avery shouted from above-deck.

"Good," Hawes called back. "Come on down."

They'd traveled a few miles south, to an abandoned pier in the old Hunter's Point Shipyard. Not the best neighborhood—arguably one of the worst in San Francisco—but they paid people here enough to look the other way where their activities were concerned.

Avery hopped off the last step, and Hawes slid to the left, making as much room as he could in the cramped cabin. Which wasn't a lot. To his left, Dante stood at the foot of the raised bed, and in front of Hawes, Lucas was passed out on the leather bench seat. He was slumped over face-down on the lacquered table, legs spread and ankles cuffed to metal posts underneath.

Not for long.

Rotating to the sink, Hawes filled a glass with water, turned back around, and chucked the cold liquid at Lucas's head.

Lucas came awake with a spluttering start, bolting upright and violently shaking his head to get rid of the water. On instinct, he tried to stand, failed, and howled when he attempted to move his broken arm in its makeshift sling.

"I'll make it hurt worse if you don't settle," Hawes said.

Lucas glared, nostrils flaring as he panted through the pain.

"You could have played dumb up there," Dante said. "Tried to cover."

"That would be an insult to them." Lucas jutted his chin at Hawes and Avery. "Kill me and get it over with. I knew the risk I was taking."

"Why'd you take it?" Hawes asked.

Lucas snapped his lips shut, determined resignation filling his eyes.

Hawes stepped forward and braced both hands on the table. It was a risk, looming over Lucas as he was, but with the operative's legs restrained, a broken arm, and all tactical weapons out of reach, there was minimal chance Lucas would reach him before Hawes could duck away.

"Who were you visiting in Big Sur last week?" he asked.

"I don't know what you're talking about."

Dante's scoff echoed Hawes's mental retort. *Now he wants to play dumb?*

Hawes said, "We have you and Avery at the same seaside inn as Jodie and Ray."

Avery gasped. "I wasn't in Big Sur last week."

"Your bank account says otherwise," Dante told her.

"Shit, I haven't checked it lately."

Even if she had, the charge might not have registered. Hawes kept his focus on Lucas. "Who was there with you using Avery's card?"

Lucas's face twisted into an unhinged grin. "Good luck figuring that one out."

Hawes cursed himself for not seeing this side of Lucas sooner. He was one of their most levelheaded operatives, a good balance to Avery's feistiness. Yes, he was an assassin, but he'd given no indication of malice or delight in the undertaking. Just cool, calm efficiency. Apparently Lucas had decided to let it all hang out, now that death was imminent.

"We can get video footage from the hotel," Dante said.

"Good luck with that too."

So they had a hacker on Team Betrayal. The same person who'd leaked the information about Papa Cal? Was that connected? A coordinated attack? Had the same hacker sent that flash drive to Dante? If so, why? For now, Hawes mentally pocketed the valuable yet disturbing nugget of information, ignored the questions it begged, and asked about another suspicion he liked even less. "You weren't going to the warehouse with the prototypes, were you?"

A single, insolent blink.

Answer enough.

Hawes pushed off the table and turned for the stairs. "Let's go."

Avery preceded him up, but Dante hung back. "That's all you're gonna ask him?"

"I got what I needed."

Dante had not. "Why'd you do it?" he asked Lucas. "Why'd you betray him?"

Hawes paused halfway up the stairs, listening for the answer.

"Because his pansy ass doesn't have the balls for this."

Ah, and there it was. Two for one, linking the organization's change of course to the fact Hawes was gay. While none of his operatives had ever expressed an issue with his sexual orientation, he'd be a fool to think there wasn't at least one homophobe among them. He'd hoped by now he'd proven his orientation didn't matter, that his ability to do the job had nothing to do with the fact that he was attracted to men, but he was a fool for hoping he'd convinced the bigots.

Hawes suspected not even Lucas getting his face bashed into the table would convince him, but Hawes appreciated Dante's gesture, the *thunk* and answering curse more than a little satisfying.

The satisfaction was short-lived. He cleared the door and came face-to-face with a pissed-off operative. Hands on her hips, Avery was livid, the halo of ringlet curls around her head only enhancing the angry-warrior effect. "Jodie and Ray weren't killed by a third-party rando, were they?"

Hawes had to proceed with caution. She'd been loyal thus far, but that was before she had the whole story, which she'd started putting together downstairs. "No, they weren't," he said.

"Did they try to kill you?"

"Yes."

"And Lucas was helping them." Not a question, a statement. "Someone used my card to make it look like I was too."

"We're going to find out who that was."

She stared him down for the few seconds it took Dante to climb the stairs and step behind him, close enough Hawes could feel his reassuring heat at his back. Two against one, though Avery's eyes never left Hawes. Dante didn't factor into the picture for her. She was judging Hawes's merit as a leader, making the decision based on what mattered here, regardless of how that played out for her life in the short term. Hawes also appreciated that.

She nodded. "I'll take care of Lucas and the prototypes. I'm here to help."

One more soldier he could count on. "Thank you." He navigated the narrow path off the boat and onto the dock. "Someone will meet you at the warehouse to help unload the prototypes."

"Sounds good," Avery said as she gathered her curls up in a bun and moved about on deck, returning to her usual self.

There was, however, a Dante-sized statue in her way. He stood, unmoving, right where Hawes had left him. Only his head rotated, looking back and forth between the cabin, Avery, and Hawes.

"We need to move," Hawes told him.

Dante hesitated another long moment before finally getting his ass in gear, clearing the stern as Avery revved the engines.

Assuming he'd follow, Hawes started down the dock for

the shore. From there, it would be another ten-minute walk before they reached a street where a Lyft would actually pick them up.

He hadn't made it far when Dante's hand clasped his arm and spun him around. "You're just going to let them go?"

"Yes."

"She's gonna kill him."

At Hawes's silence, frustration flared in Dante's eyes, same as it had last night. Except Hawes was close enough to do something about it this time. He wrenched his arm free and hooked his right leg behind Dante's left. Surprise, and the threat of water on either side of them, gave Hawes the advantage. Enough that it outweighed the lingering stiffness in his back. He grabbed Dante's flailing arm and shifted them so Dante's back hit a pier pylon, catching them both. He pressed up against Dante, the precarious balance working in his favor. "Lucas betrayed me, and he betrayed Avery. She'll do her job." Dante cast his gaze aside, and Hawes grasped his chin, hauling it back. "Don't forget who I am, Mr. Perry."

"The Prince."

"Of Killers."

Still hated it. And still needed it, especially where this man was concerned, an unknown variable in a rising sea of unknowns. Hawes sensed this one was more dangerous than all the rest. A rip current of need was already tugging at him, threatening to drag him under, offering tempting relief. It was all he could do not to slide his fingers along Dante's stubbled jaw, not to shove his hand into all that hair, not to lean forward and claim his mouth. Not to rub against the hardness pressing into his thigh.

Hawes dropped his hand and rocked back a step. "I demand loyalty."

Dante pushed off the pole, erasing the distance between them. "I'm here to help." A mirror of Avery's earlier words, yet the layers beneath Dante's utterance were endless.

Hawes fought the pull, forced himself to turn, and started back down the pier. "Call us a Lyft," he tossed over his shoulder, not letting Dante witness the waves of contradictory emotions crashing over him. He felt more in control than he had the past twenty-four hours. He'd rooted out another traitor, extracted useful information, and secured the loyalty of one of his best soldiers. Yet another part of him, buried deep beneath the suits and locked-down demeanor, wanted to let go, wanted to go wild, for Dante.

EIGHT

They sat around a table in one of the hospice house parlors —Hawes shuffling a deck of cards, Helena and Holt tapping at their handheld devices, and Amelia breast-feeding Lily. Hawes riffled the cards once more, cut the deck, dealt them into four stacks, and distributed one to each player.

Helena picked up her cards. "It's consistent with what we know so far," she said, continuing the conversation from where Hawes had left off telling them about Lucas.

Amelia shifted Lily and picked up her stack. She fanned the cards with her nimble fingers, glanced over them once, then laid the spread stack back on the table, facedown. "Maybe I could have gotten more out of him."

"Doubt it," Helena said as she arranged her own cards. "No incentive if he knew he wasn't getting off that boat."

Holt didn't look up from his cards. "So it's an operative in my shop, given what Lucas implied about the wiped footage."

"Not necessarily." Hawes did the same card arrangement dance as his siblings. Papa Cal had taught them all to play Hearts, and in doing so, how to hold and play their cards, which made the pass fairly predictable.

Except for Amelia who, one-handed, chose her pass cards from where she'd last seen them and slid them to Holt. "It could be an outside hacker."

Holt shot her a glare, twice-over.

She smiled back at him in a way only she could get away with. "You are not the be-all-end-all of hackers, sweetheart."

"Local FBI's had two as good as you," Helena said.

"Who?" Holt scoffed. "Baller and Barbie?"

Helena muffled a laugh. "Never let her hear you call her that, or you won't have any balls left."

Amelia patted Holt's cheek. "She's right, and I love your balls, so don't."

Holt rolled his eyes, and Hawes laughed too, improbable as it was in this place, but so too was this discussion. That said, it was a distraction from the truth at the end of the hallway that none of them wanted to face. So, family hour at the hospice house had turned into a debrief.

"Besides, they're the good guys," Hawes said. "We know it's not them."

Helena threw down the two of clubs, starting the round. "And this looks more and more like an inside job."

"Start with your shop," Hawes said to Holt. "If you find nothing, branch out. It could be someone inside hiring out." They went for several tricks before Hawes spoke again. "Dante's right. We need to flush them out."

"We need to keep a low profile," Helena countered. "Brax is doing what he can, but there's only so far we can push. We got lucky this morning."

Because Lucas moved those explosives out at the last possible second.

"You sure the prototypes weren't there for SFPD's benefit?" Amelia asked. *And to our family's detriment,* she didn't need to say.

"They were definitely headed somewhere else," Hawes said.

While Lucas hadn't flat out said it, Hawes was confident Lucas had been equally motivated to get those explosives out before they were discovered.

"I'll check the dark web." Holt glumly collected another trick from the middle of the table. Despite being a genius at ones and zeroes, he was terrible at cards. He refused to count them, even though he could, and strategy was not his strong suit. "Let me see if anyone's put a call out."

Helena's phone vibrated on the table. She turned it over and glanced at the screen. "Speaking of putting a call out..." She slid the device to Hawes. "You may recall you assigned Jodie and Ray this one last month, after that shitshow of a trial."

The request had come in directly to Helena, Holt had vetted it, and Hawes had signed off on the job. That was before they were trying to keep a low profile. "Shit," Hawes cursed low. "He took the bait?"

"The meet is scheduled for three a.m.," Helena said.

Hawes threw down his last card and reclined in his chair, balancing on the two back legs, playing out the options in his head while the others finished the round. They could not afford extra attention right now, not when they were still reeling from last night. They also couldn't afford to pass up this opportunity. But who could he assign? No one else was up to speed on the contract or on the need for extra caution. The only people who had the full story, who could do this right, were him and the people at the table with him.

Holt cleared the last trick from the center of the table, and Hawes brought his chair back down. "We do it," he said, gesturing to the four of them. "We know all the variables in play."

"It's what Papa Cal would want," Helena said softly.

Hawes couldn't agree more. They owed their grandfather this much, for the legacy he was leaving them.

As if summoned by the mention of her husband, Rose appeared in the doorway. She looked like a shell of her normal polished self. Gray hair falling out of its French braid, her usually manicured nails chipped, weariness weighing down her shoulders. Hawes had seen her like this one other time. When she'd arrived home, weary from weeks on the run, to news that her son and daughter-in-law, Hawes's parents, were dead. It had been the final straw then, momentarily breaking her. Hawes feared they were fast approaching another such moment now. His fear and certainty ratcheted up when a somber doctor appeared behind her.

Hawes rose and moved to stand next to Helena. "What's going on?"

"Your grandfather has taken a turn for the worse," the doctor said.

Rose drove it the rest of the way home. "He's not asking for your parents anymore. He says Noah and Charlotte are there in the room, waiting for him."

Helena muffled a cry and reached for Hawes's hand. Across from them, Holt wrapped his wife and daughter in his arms, burying his face in Amelia's hair. Rose collapsed onto the arm of the nearest chair and covered her face with her hands, sobbing quietly.

Dread settled in Hawes's gut, on his aching back, and fuck if the crushing weight bearing down on him didn't feel like the heaviest straw known to man.

Hawes turned the corner onto his street and spotted the Hog parked out front, its polished chrome and pearlescent blue paint gleaming in the halo of the streetlight. And leaning against a nearby lamppost, reading a new book, was the bike's owner. Not hiding anymore.

"You making this a habit?" Hawes asked as he approached.

Dante pushed off the pole, tucked his book under his arm, and met Hawes in front of the building's steps. The PI had changed since that morning. Jeans and a tank again, this one gray, and his denim jacket had been traded for a battered leather duster. Hawes bet the soft-looking leather smelled amazing, years of life worn into its grain. One of a kind.

"When do you get your Benz back?" Dante asked.

Not one of a kind, aside from a few custom modifications. Generic, relatively. "When Kane decides to release it from the impound lot." If Hawes decided to reclaim it at all. He was leaning toward donating it to charity instead.

"Anything else from him today?" Dante asked as they made their way to the stairs.

"Nothing, though I haven't been back to the office since Holt and I left to visit Papa Cal midday."

"It's past ten. Where've you been?"

"Ballpark." He'd missed most of the game, arriving during the seventh-inning stretch, but after hours at the hospice house, with only Lily's whimpers to break the heavy silence that had settled over his family, Hawes had needed to zone out with baseball and a beer.

"Before that, Madigan."

"You don't know?" Hawes thumbed the sensor by his door, entered his code on the keypad, and once the door unlocked, pushed inside. "You seem to know everything. To be everywhere." The sudden spike of irritation surprised Hawes but didn't stop him from rounding on Dante with his own query. "Where have *you* been, if you weren't following me?"

Dante raised his hands, palms out. "Working on my end of this, then had dinner with my family." He stood outside the door, waiting for Hawes to invite him in.

Smart. And enough time for Hawes to consider and dismiss the usual concerns. Dante had already spent an evening at his place, had had his back today at the office and with Lucas, and when it boiled right down to it, Hawes didn't want to be alone tonight. He waved Dante inside.

"I didn't follow you because I'm not your keeper," Dante said as he closed the door. "You don't need one, as you keep demonstrating. You seem tense, is all, for having come from a game the Giants won."

Guess he hadn't zoned out as well as he'd hoped. A stiffer drink, then. Hawes shrugged out of his suit coat, flung it toward the loft stairs, and made his way into the living room. Iris wove around his ankles, demanding attention, and he bent to give her a scratch. Once she moved on to Dante, Hawes righted himself and opened the built-in minibar in the cabinet next to the desk. He retrieved the squat bottle of Crown Royal Rye and two shot glasses.

"Would've figured you for a Macallan guy." Dante skirted behind him, his knuckles brushing the curve of Hawes's ass. "Something classier," Dante continued as he rounded the couch and collapsed onto the middle cushion.

Hawes stood frozen. Intentional or not, Dante's grazing touch had sent electricity crackling up his spine. If Dante had stopped behind him, if he'd rotated his hand the other way and cupped Hawes's ass, Hawes wouldn't have been able to stop himself from leaning into the promise of that touch.

Fuck, he was all over the place. Angry. Frightened. Impatient. Frustrated, in more than one respect. Not even the unusual steadying effect Dante had on him was working tonight.

Whisky and glasses in hand, Hawes closed the cabinet with his elbow. "One, this was world whisky of the year a few years back, and two, the expensive stuff is wasted on me." He sank onto the cushion next to Dante. "I don't drink enough to appreciate the difference. This or Jameson serves my purpose just fine."

Dante relieved him of the glasses. "To get drunk?"

"Basically." Hawes removed the decorative cork and poured them generous shots. He took his glass from Dante, threw back the shot, then poured another before setting the bottle on the coffee table. "Hospice visit took longer than anticipated."

"Complications with Papa Cal?"

"Obviously." Hawes winced at his snappish tone.

Dante didn't flinch, but his gaze was more assessing than usual. "I'm not the enemy here."

"How do I know that?"

The staredown that followed lasted a good half minute, until Dante broke it to toss back his shot. His lips puckered, then parted as he let out a sharp gasp, a common response to the spicy rye. Hawes's nearly blinding need to throw a leg over Dante's lap and swallow that gasp with his own mouth was not so common. He wasn't sure he'd ever felt a spike of desire so strong.

Before Hawes could act on it, Dante removed the option by shifting forward to the edge of the couch. He set his empty glass on the table next to the bottle, then did the same with all his weapons, removing them one by one. Glock. Knife. Handcuffs. Tactical pen. Book, the next in the series. He took off his coat too and emptied his pockets. Keys, wallet, and phone.

"There," he said. "I'm unarmed now." He slid back, stretched an arm along the top of the couch, and crossed a long leg toward Hawes. "You and I both know you could take me either way, but for your peace of mind…"

Hawes chuckled bitterly. "I'm not sure even this"—he lifted his glass—"will give me peace of mind tonight." Slumping into the soft cushions, Hawes sipped his second shot more slowly, savoring the burn on his tongue and down his throat. He imagined it melting away the glaciers that had flowed near the center of his chest today. Impossible, of course, as the first of those ice blocks had been formed almost two decades ago.

He finished the whisky and rested his head on top of the cushion, staring at the ceiling. Counting planks and light fixtures brought him no peace either. "Right now, I'm pretty sure I couldn't take anyone."

"How bad is he?" Dante said, accurately reading his distress.

"He told Rose that my parents are there, waiting for him in the room." Hawes closed his eyes and recounted more of what the doctor had told them. "He's not eating anymore, after he choked multiple times over the weekend. His body can't even remember how to function properly."

Dante tugged Hawes's glass free from his hand and set it on the table. He scooted closer, judging by the fragrant waft of eucalyptus shampoo and the nearness of his lowered voice. "It's a terrible disease."

Hawes rotated his head and opened his eyes, meeting Dante's sympathetic brown ones only a few inches away. "You know someone?"

"Uncle. He was this big Italian guy with a huge personality to match. Best cook in the family, and we've got a lot of good ones." His unfocused eyes drifted over Hawes's shoulder. "Saw him tonight. He's lost half his weight, barely spoke to anyone, and struggled to remember the family lasagna recipe."

Hawes laid a hand on Dante's knee, briefly, before yanking it back, not trusting himself to resist the temptation to slide it higher. Not the time. He folded his hands in his lap. "No matter how much money we throw at it, Alzheimer's kills faster than we can keep up with it."

"You throw a lot at it, don't you? Annual donations the past three years to charities that support Alzheimer's research and to others that fund shelters for LGBTQ youth."

"I don't need all the money my trust provides. I used what I needed"—he gestured at their surroundings—"and found better uses for the rest."

Dante lifted a hand and brushed back the overlong top

hairs that were tickling Hawes's forehead. "Careful, Madigan. Your soul is showing."

Hawes's eyes slipped shut as Dante's fingers lingered on his temple. Finally, the calm steadiness he'd missed washed over him. Be it from Dante's touch or the whisky, Hawes couldn't say, but he didn't pull away, unwilling to disturb the peace. "Some prince," he mumbled.

"King, before long."

And hello disturbance. A chasm opened beneath Hawes's feet, knocking him back off-balance. He stood and stepped away to avoid it. "What if I don't want to be?"

"A killer?"

"The king." Hawes locked his hands behind his head and paced the area on the other side of the coffee table. "I don't want to be king. Not if I have to destroy my soul again to do it."

Dante uncrossed his legs and shifted forward, elbows on his knees. "Again?"

"I have the health care power of attorney. I ultimately have to make the decision if it comes to life support." Hawes braced himself against the side of the ladder. "Again." He closed his eyes against the flood of memories, and when that didn't work, buried his face in his arm.

Dante caught on a second later and was up and off the couch, his footsteps short and fast, drawing closer with speed instead of his usual casual lope. A hand landed on Hawes's hip, Dante's voice and heat close. "You made the decision about your parents too, didn't you?"

"My grandparents were out of town, laying low at one of the safe houses." He swallowed hard. "I was sixteen."

"Jesus, Hawes." Dante slid his arm the rest of the way around Hawes's waist in a loose sideways hug. He snuck his other hand under Hawes's chin, nudging until Hawes lifted his face enough to cup his cheek. "What do you need?"

"I don't want to be in control." No decisions to make, no kingdom to rule, no bad guys to sort from the good. Tonight, freedom was the most settling thought there was, especially if it involved the man whose body was pressed alongside his.

"Do you trust me?" Dante said.

Hawes half nodded, half nuzzled Dante's palm.

"Give it to me, then."

Hawes's eyes popped open, and an unexpected laugh bubbled out of him. "I'm not giving you control of my family's empire."

One corner of Dante's mouth turned up in a sexy smirk. "I don't want that either." With his arm around Hawes's waist, he shifted them so they were in front of the ladder, Hawes's back against the rungs, Dante's body blanketing his. The pressure, front and back, massaged away any lingering soreness from Ray's hit last night. Not that Hawes would care when Dante's long, strong fingers were skirting up the side of his face and into his hair, threading through the strands and cradling his scalp.

Hawes couldn't look away, couldn't stop his hands from curling into Dante's gray tank and hauling him closer. "Please."

"I want control of you." Dante's soft lips brushed the sharp right hinge of Hawes's jaw. "Let me help you." He moved to the other side. "Let me make you forget for a while." Then to the crease at the bottom of Hawes's chin. "Let go for me."

Yes.

Hawes lowered his face the half inch needed to bring their lips together. And let go. Of the last twenty-four hours. Of the control he'd exercised over family, company, and fate today. Of himself, where Dante was concerned.

He parted his lips on a groan, and Dante swept inside, grazing teeth and tongue, and Hawes relished the attention, the invasion. He parried, sucked, and opened wider, angling to give Dante better access. Ripe for plunder, Hawes wanted nothing more than to be laid bare. He'd gladly surrender to Dante's devouring mouth. To Dante's warm, hard body blanketing every inch of his cold, sharp one. To his hips rocking an impressive erection against the one straining behind Hawes's zipper.

Lost in the best kiss he'd had in years, Hawes didn't register Dante grasping his wrists and lifting his arms above his head, not until Dante broke the kiss and curled Hawes's fingers around the ladder rung. "Don't let go."

Hawes chased after Dante's mouth. "I thought that's what I was supposed to be doing."

"I want you to hang on," Dante whispered against his lips. "And let go for me."

Yes.

Hawes was glad for the handhold when Dante's lips skated off his mouth and traveled to his earlobe, nipping and tugging with his teeth. Knees weak, Hawes was half tempted to ditch standing altogether and hike his legs around Dante's waist. The better to grind his cock against those abs. The stray thought vanished as soon as Dante moved from nipping his earlobe to tracing the shell of his ear with his tongue, from the narrow top, down to the lobe again, and behind it. As if the tongue wasn't enough torture, the scruff of Dante's beard lit the surrounding area on fire.

"God, yes, more like that." Hawes rested his head on another rung, rolling it side to side so Dante could kiss and lick every inch of his throat. He didn't give a flying fuck if the occasional suck and nip left marks. And when Dante's tongue dipped into the crook of his neck, the groove made deeper by his pronounced clavicle, Hawes also didn't give a flying fuck if the neighbors heard him scream.

"Yes, fuck, yes!"

Dante grinned. "Sensitive spot?"

Hawes lowered a hand and tangled it in Dante's hair, the silky strands gliding through his fingers. He twisted them around his fist, holding Dante right where he wanted him. "Again," he tried to order, tried to voice his desire, but between his strangled voice and the desperate rutting of his cock against Dante's, the speed of which had increased with each kiss, his order came out closer to a plea.

Dante indulged him for one more dip of his tongue, one more nip of teeth, before he dropped a light kiss over the tortured skin. A shiver raced through Hawes. Dante chased it away with the molten look in his eyes and the gravel in his voice. "Who's in control here?"

Challenge flared deep inside Hawes. The instinct to fight back was there, where earlier it had wavered. Dante had stoked it back to life by taking the reins. Wanting that flame to burn brighter, Hawes untangled his hand and lifted it back to the rung. Holding on and letting go, letting someone else drive so he could just feel, ceding control so he could regain it.

Dante rewarded him for the power given, starting with the top button of Hawes's dress shirt and ending with the last. He kissed and licked every inch of exposed skin until he was on his knees, hands unfastening Hawes's pants while his tongue rimmed Hawes's belly button.

Like Hawes wanted him to rim a different hole. He closed his eyes, drowning in sensation. The pleasure intensified as Dante shoved down his pants and exposed his hip bones. Dante flared his fingers over them, tracing and teasing.

"Careful," Hawes said. "They cut."

"You are a pointy bastard." Yet Dante didn't seem remotely scared of Hawes's sharp edges, tongue following in the path of his hands, all the way down to the patch of light-brown hair at the end of the trail above Hawes's cock, which was woefully trapped beneath the waistband of his boxers.

Hand slipping off the rail again, Hawes pinched his puckered nipple, aiming to redirect his focus before he came in his shorts like a teenager.

Dante helped him out, yanking down the damnable boxers and finally freeing his cock. Hawes moaned in relief, then frustration, as Dante rose and stepped away, save for a single finger that traced the underside of Hawes's erection.

"Do you want me to leave you here like this, cock out, hard and aching?" Dante circled the head and pressed lightly at Hawes's slit, spreading the moisture there. "Dripping." Abruptly, Dante removed his hand and took another step back. He gripped himself through his jeans.

Hawes groaned at the length and girth on display, making his mouth water and his asshole clench. He wanted it in both. He squeezed his nipple, hard, one last time, then put his hand back where it belonged.

"Better." Dante closed the distance again, his smile

predatory, and pressed his upturned lips to Hawes's, plunging into his mouth once more. Hand between them, he palmed the underside of Hawes's cock, moving it into position, and rutted his own against it, the denim friction sending Hawes's senses into overdrive.

"Oh God, too much," Hawes keened against his lips. "Too—"

Dante leaned far enough back to meet his eyes. Concern cooled the burning desire there. "Is it too much? I can stop."

Hawes shook his head. "No, good idea. Just intense."

"If it's ever not, if you need control back—"

"Sunshine." It had been his safe word whenever he'd played with past partners.

Dante smiled and rested their foreheads together. "Don't like the daylight?"

Hawes twisted enough to run his nose down Dante's cheek, inhaling his scent and reveling in the rough texture of his scruff. "Grew up in the fog."

Dante angled his face in turn, capturing Hawes's mouth for a kiss that stole his breath. That sent wispy tentacles of tangled emotions creeping through Hawes's veins, aimed for other more tender places. Hawes didn't bother to sort it out right then, not with Dante dropping again to his knees. He didn't waste time tracing the same path with his tongue that his finger had traveled earlier. He closed his mouth around Hawes's cock and swallowed him to the root.

Yes.

Hawes closed his eyes and held on tight. Letting go of everything and giving himself to Dante. Getting lost in the fog had never felt so good.

NINE

Hawes crept down the loft stairs in darkness, not needing light to take care of the basics—relieve his bladder, brush his teeth, pop a few ibuprofen, don a dark suit with multiple layers so he could change outfits if necessary, and arm himself. Not expecting a fight, he pocketed a garrote and strapped a single knife around his calf under his pant leg.

A text from Helena lit up his phone screen. **5 minutes**.

Hawes deleted the message, pocketed the phone along with his wallet and keys, and closed things up. He followed the faint trail of moonlight into the living area. Dante was stretched out on the couch, a book splayed facedown on his steadily moving chest, his light snores echoed by Iris's purrs. The traitor was curled up on his feet. She blinked once at Hawes, yellow eyes acknowledging his presence, then went back to ignoring him in favor of her new human pillow.

A pillow Hawes would've liked to curl up with too, if Dante would've let him. Instead, once Hawes had returned to earth after the best blowjob of his life, Dante had insisted he go to bed. Alone. Maybe it had something to do with Hawes dozing off against the ladder in his postorgasmic haze. He would have rallied for the chance to return the favor, but Dante had taken that possibility off the table. Hawes had been too tired to argue, and now time was too tight. He wanted to run his fingers through the long hair fanned out over the pillow, wanted to throw a leg around Dante's waist and stretch out over the length of him, wanted to steal a long, slow kiss. Wanted to taste all of him. Unfortunately, he couldn't do any of those things if he wanted to get out of there on time, and without waking Dante.

Leaving him there was a risk, but one Hawes was willing to take for the warmth that bloomed in his chest at the mere thought. He also liked the thought of Dante with him on the job. He could be an asset to them, but Hawes, clearheaded after a few hours of sleep, couldn't ignore the fact that he'd only known Dante a little over a day and that Holt hadn't finished vetting him. While those facts hadn't stopped Hawes from giving over his body last night, or from leaving Dante at his condo now, it did keep him from bringing Dante further into the fold.

Other than the kill he'd witnessed in the alley, Dante had no eyes-on proof of what Hawes and his family did for a second living. And as for the alley, they were even, Hawes having witnessed Dante's kill as well. Mutually assured destruction. But Dante hadn't seen the rest of Hawes's family in action, and Hawes wasn't about to risk them too.

His phone vibrated in his pocket. Time was up. Iris gave him another blink, and Hawes put a finger to his lips, shushing her. He scratched behind her ears and took one last lingering look at Dante. Not a bad sight before leaving for work.

Downstairs, a nondescript sedan waited at the curb, Helena behind the wheel, Amelia in the passenger seat. They didn't look like they'd gotten much sleep either.

"You good?" Amelia asked as he slid into the back seat.

He nodded and asked after Holt.

"Better," his brother answered out of the car speakers. "Now that Lily's finally down."

"You need more time?"

"Don't have more time," Helena cut in. "We're already late." She was tense. Jobs like the one tonight tended to do that to her. As an attorney who specialized in freeing the wrongfully accused, Helena took the cases of the wrongfully acquitted personally. Which fit well with Hawes's realignment of the organization. He and Helena were on the same page regarding targets.

"Everything's in place," Amelia said as she handed him a tablet. "Jodie and Ray did a good job on the setup."

Hawes scrolled through the assembled case file on Walter Campbell III. Late-forties, white, rich, well-connected. Involved in local politics until he'd been accused of sexually abusing teen boys he'd met via a government-sponsored mentorship program. The charges hadn't stuck. That's what happened when traumatized teens overdosed on Gray Death, fentanyl-laced heroin popular on the streets; when witnesses changed their stories before they could testify; and when the abuser was fraternity brothers with the judge who tried his case. Not the same chapter, so supposedly there was no conflict of interest. Hawes called bullshit.

"Who does he think he's meeting tonight?"

"A fifteen-year-old kid he picked up online," Amelia answered.

Hawes read through the emails between Campbell and a person he thought was an underage boy. Ray had been working him for weeks, encouraging Campbell's promises of money and drugs. In reality, all Campbell ever left in his wake were bruises, addiction, and suicides. Hawes hoped there was an afterlife so this asshole could appreciate the irony of what was about to befall him.

"Jodie and Ray warned him?" Another of Hawes's new-order conditions.

"Three different times," Holt answered. "And I locked down his computer. Fucker hired one of *my kids* to go around it." Holt's "kids" were the homeless teens at the LGBTQ shelter Hawes regularly donated to and where Holt also volunteered his time teaching programming. The kids worshiped Holt, were loyal to him before anyone else, and Holt protected them like he'd protected Hawes growing up. This had to rankle.

"We're here," Helena said as she parked in the staff lot behind one of the Tendernob's trendy new hotels. Classy enough for Campbell's standards, not so classy as to draw attention, and close to his marks.

"Camera is going on loop in…" Holt's rapid-fire typing pinged through the speakers. "Three, two, one." The typing stopped. "You've got ten minutes."

Helena tugged on her gloves. "Plenty of time."

Words were at a minimum as they unfolded from the car and slipped through the hotel's open back door. Amelia shoved a wad of cash into the hand of the waiting night manager, who also confirmed all the rooms around Campbell's were empty. They took the service elevator up to the fifth floor, where Hawes and Helena waited, peeking around the corner as Amelia approached Campbell's door.

Her willowy figure was striking in a black trench, little black dress, and elbow-length gloves. Taken together with her alabaster skin, long dark hair, and bright green eyes, she made an effective Trojan horse on operations. She also wasn't in the public eye as much as Hawes or Helena, making it easier for her to take on personas and get a foot in the door. Assuming she could get the door open. After Campbell ignored her first few knocks, she slipped a folded note under the door. It opened a moment later.

"Good evening, Mr. Campbell."

He looked taken aback, surprised she'd used his real name. He'd used an alias in the emails Hawes had skimmed. Campbell glanced down at the note, then back up. "I'm sorry," he stuttered, "I was expecting... I didn't know he had a..."

"Pimp," Amelia said. "That's the word you're looking for. And you're a John."

"I'm not—"

She talked over his futile protest. "I meet all the new Johns first. Make sure everything is settled."

Campbell's wrinkled forehead smoothed out. "You're here to collect."

Blinded by her smile, Campbell held open the door and let her in. She kicked the rubber stopper into place, propping the door slightly ajar.

Hawes and Helena crept around the corner to either side of the door.

"I was worried for a moment," Campbell said. "I speci-fied certain—"

"I know what you wanted."

"As do we." Helena stepped into the room ahead of Hawes, who closed the door behind them. "Even if the justice system doesn't believe it."

"But now," Hawes said, "everyone will know the truth by morning, after you confess your crimes and commit suicide."

Campbell made a break for the door. Stupid, as there were three people between him and it. Instincts were instincts, though, and Campbell was bigger than all three of them. He probably thought he could barrel right over them, but he was nowhere near as quick as he'd been in his college running back days. It took less than a minute to wrestle him into the desk chair and strap down his limbs.

"Who are you?" he croaked, voice trembling.

"Do you remember Adam Wilson?" Hawes said.

"Who?"

Helena, standing behind the chair, reached over his shoulder and opened his laptop. "Log in," she ordered.

"No, you can't make—"

"Oh yes, we can make you." Amelia's gloved hand hit a pressure point that made Campbell howl. She didn't stop until he logged in and the desktop appeared.

"There's a file waiting for you. *My Crimes.*" Hawes traded places with Helena and reached around Campbell. He clicked the mouse until Adam's picture appeared. "That's Adam Wilson."

"I don't remember him from the trial," Campbell said.

"Because he's dead," Helena said. "You plied a fifteen-year-old kid with Gray Death, got him hooked on you and the drug, and when you found a shinier toy, you left him high and dry. He overdosed on the parting gift you left him."

"That's not the name he gave me. I thought he was a professional!"

Hawes spun his chair around and braced his gloved hands on the armrests, getting in Campbell's face. "That doesn't make it okay, you sick fuck."

At Campbell's side, Amelia hit another pressure point, and tears sprang to his eyes. "I'm sorry. I didn't know who he was," he cried through the pain.

Hawes shoved back, and Helena stepped back in, her blue eyes burning with cold fury. "His father didn't want to tarnish his memory with that farce of a trial. You were never going to be convicted. Not when you're a former city supervisor and fraternity brothers with the judge. He should have recused himself, and you should be behind bars."

"I can pay you," Campbell tried to bargain. "Or swing a city favor your way."

"We don't need those things from you," Helena hissed and spun his chair back around. "No one needs you at all."

Standing at the side of the desk, Hawes rotated the laptop toward him, found the confession Holt had uploaded into the *My Crimes* folder, and opened up the electronic signature app. "Sign it."

He hesitated, and Hawes thought of Lucas. Campbell's incentive was withering by the second. He mentally reviewed Campbell's bio. No wife and kids, but... Hawes turned from the desk to Campbell's bag in the corner. It only took a few seconds to find what he was looking for. Fucking amateur. "You have a twelve-year-old nephew," he said, returning to face off against Campbell across the desk. He tossed the drug paraphernalia and baggie of Gray Death onto the middle of it. "Wonder what he'd do, if he found that just lying around?" Hawes would never do such a thing, but Campbell didn't know that.

The leverage worked. Campbell signed the confession, and Amelia snatched up the baggie and supplies. Elastic to tie off his arm, a syringe, a lighter, and a spoon.

"Oh God," Campbell whimpered as she expertly set up everything.

"Pretty sure God wants nothing to do with you either," Hawes said as Helena tied the tourniquet around his arm.

Amelia filled the syringe. "Were you really going to shoot a kid up with this stuff?"

"Wait, wait," Campbell hollered, still clutching at survival straws. "I have information."

"I doubt it's anything we don't already know," Hawes said.

"You're under investigation."

Hawes's blood ran cold. Jodie's and Ray's deaths had been kept out of the news. So how did Campbell know about it? Or was this about the winery or warehouse? Or a different investigation altogether? He held up a hand, and Amelia paused, the syringe an inch from Campbell's vein. "You have to give us more than that," Hawes said.

"There was a sealed document on the judge's desk last month. I saw your company's name."

Not Jodie and Ray, then. Nor the warehouse or winery. Something else. And there'd been something even more important in Campbell's words. Hawes sprang the trap. "What name was that?"

Campbell blanched and snapped shut his mouth, realizing his mistake too late.

"You know who we are."

Campbell remained mute, but his terrified eyes, and his

earlier words, said it all. Still, Hawes had to be sure. He nodded at Amelia and Helena.

Amelia withdrew the syringe, and Helena pulled back Campbell's pinky finger far enough to cause pain but not a break. That wouldn't fit the picture they were creating. "Who are we?" his sister demanded.

"Madigan!" Campbell cried, his eyes never leaving Hawes. "Hawes Madigan."

"You should have kept that bit to yourself." Hawes circled the desk. "Now you're definitely not getting out of here alive. Not that there'd been a chance before." He held out a hand to Amelia, and she laid the syringe in his palm. "Do you know what they call me?"

Campbell shook his head, and the sweat from the ends of his hair joined the tears streaming down his face.

"The Prince of Killers." This was one of those rare times Hawes liked the moniker. Not just its usefulness as a deterrent, like at the warehouse, but for the terror it brought to the guilty eyes of those who'd put fear in the eyes of innocents. *This* was why he did what he did. When justice failed, Hawes and his family righted the balance. He was happy to rule this kingdom, as prince or king.

He found the protruding vein in Campbell's arm and pressed the tip of the syringe to it, breaking the skin.

"Wait, please!" Campbell cried.

"Justice has waited long enough." Hawes pressed the plunger.

TEN

Hawes took the stairs up to Holt's lair two at a time. It was still dark outside, and inside most of the house was too, except for the light filtering down from the brightly lit upper level. Holt had no doubt been running on all cylinders since they'd briefed him in the car about Campbell's nebulous warning.

"What do we know?" Hawes asked as he crested the top stair.

"That you've got a problem."

The answer, voiced by the last person Hawes expected, came from the far corner of the room. His grandmother sat in the rocker, a sleeping Lily in her arms, a cat on each foot, as if they'd conspired to never let her leave again. If that was the case... "Papa Cal?" Hawes asked, fearing the worst.

"Not yet." Rose closed her eyes and held Lily closer. "I needed to come home and check back in with reality." She reopened her eyes and pinned Hawes to the spot. "And what do I find? A mess."

She always could make Hawes feel like he was doing it all wrong. She didn't break out that imperious tone often, but when she did, nine times out of ten she was right. That was how Hawes had learned many of his most valuable lessons. He hated to think of her worried about the family and business now, when she was days from losing her husband. He unstuck himself and crossed the room. He bent to kiss Lily's head, then Rose's cheek. "We'll handle it. You don't need to worry—"

"Please," she said, patting his cheek. "Let me worry about something else for five minutes." She held his stare, and in her familiar blue gaze was the same determination Helena had had in her eyes earlier tonight.

"All right." He grasped her hand, squeezing it as he stepped to her side. "We've got a problem. The more brains the better, especially yours."

Holt spun from his bank of computers and turned his face up for Amelia's quick kiss. There were bags under his brown eyes, and his wide shoulders were slumped under the flannel. It looked like he'd slept less than Hawes lately. "I can't find any filed docs from a month ago regarding any investigation."

"Did you call Kane?" Hawes asked.

"Three times. He's not returning my calls."

"He's not our enemy here."

"That's impossible," Rose said. "He's the police. We run an illegal operation. Don't forget that."

Hawes didn't think Kane could ever truly be their enemy, but Rose was right. Their interests, for the most part, were at odds.

"I have court contacts I can work," Helena said. "I'll have better luck in the morning, in person."

"Do we have any idea what this is about?" Rose asked.

"He said the company was under investigation," Helena answered. "It could be law enforcement or the health department, for all we know."

"I'm running a comprehensive sweep," Holt said. "Filings, searches, flags, assignments. If it's on a government computer, I'll find it."

An investigation, on top of trying to find a traitor, the latter of which Hawes hadn't told Rose about yet. That was an additional stressor she didn't need. It didn't appear the two matters were connected, though Hawes couldn't dismiss the possibility. Pull one string, and who knew how many others would unravel. Would he have any clothes left when he took the throne? Which would be any day now, and his family was looking to him to make sure the kingdom prevailed.

"Okay, order of attack," he said. "Holt, stay on top of the searches. Amelia, make sure he sleeps some too."

She kissed her husband's head. "I'm on it."

"I'll work our health department contacts," Hawes continued. "Helena, you work the legal, and if you're near the station—"

"I'll make sure Brax gets a visit too," she said with a smile.

"Are we expecting any blowback from the job tonight?" Rose asked.

Hawes shook his head. "It'll get media attention, but all went according to plan. It'll look like suicide. Won't be tied to us."

"All right, just one more thing, then. What are we going to do about your new shadow?" She nodded at the surveillance feed of the hallway outside his condo.

All quiet, no sign of Dante.

"Has he left?" Hawes asked Holt.

"Negative." Holt flipped the footage over to the front of the building. Dante's bike was still parked under the streetlamp. "Unless he went out the balcony doors, but the security system reports no doors or windows opened since you left."

Hawes checked his watch. Almost two hours ago now. Almost a day and a half since Dante Perry had sauntered into his life. Was the PI pulling a string too? Or helping to hold the fabric together? Hawes had certainly felt unraveled last night. The good kind, though, that had helped him relax and sleep for a few hours before this morning's job. But one of Dante's motives couldn't be argued—he had admitted to using them. As such, Hawes felt no guilt using him too.

"Continue as if he's a potential threat," Hawes said to Holt. Caution was warranted. "Did you find any payments? Any connection to Isabelle? She meant something to him. Their paths had to have crossed."

"Not that I can find. And no one's paying him to be here or to investigate us. I tracked his recent deposits, and everything lines up with completed jobs."

"But something else doesn't," Helena said, her skepticism unwavering.

Hawes couldn't deny there were holes in Dante's story that required filling. "Keep digging," he said. "I'll proceed as if he's a source. See if he knows about the investigation Campbell mentioned." He gestured at the monitors. "Keep tabs on him after. I want to see if he takes the information and runs to someone." Authorities or traitors.

"Should we keep the meet today?" Holt asked. "If the buyer gets wind of anything amiss…"

"Canceling would be a bigger red flag." Except under one circumstance, which anyone, including their buyer, would understand. "Unless we need to cancel to be with you and Papa Cal," he said to Rose.

She shook her head. "You're right. You need to go ahead with the meet." Her approval quieted Hawes's doubts. "The last thing Callum would want is for the organization to stop running because of him."

It was also the last thing Hawes wanted. What they'd done that morning mattered; they needed to keep doing it. He might not have agreed with Papa Cal's reign of terror, or his parents' robotic efficiency, but with Holt and Helena by his side, and Amelia and Rose on board, he could shape the organization into something that worked for this generation and their legacy. Something for good.

Hawes emerged from the entry hall and stared at the gorgeous, hilarious sight in front of him. "She's got you trained already."

Dante spread his arms where he sat at the dining table. He looked hotter than he had any right to—olive skin glowing in the morning light, hair in a messy top knot, a book in one hand and a spoon in the other. That was the gorgeous part. The hilarious part was Iris's back paws on his denim-clad thighs, her front ones on the table, and her face in his cereal bowl. "She didn't give me a chance to finish." He tossed his book on the table. "Just jumped right up and claimed it for herself."

"That's my fault." Laughing, Hawes followed his nose to the pot of coffee in the kitchen. "I don't like cereal milk, so she always gets mine."

"You don't like cereal milk?" Dante gasped. "What kind of monster are you?"

"I don't know." He filled a mug with coffee, sipped the life-giving brew, and leaned a hip against the island. "You've had four hours here alone. You tell me. What monstrous things did you find?"

"Only one that was truly evil." He shooed Iris off his lap, stood, and pulled a cookbook out of the many on the buffet table. Hawes suspected he knew which one. Dante brought it over to the island and tossed it onto the granite countertop.

Suspicion confirmed. *Cooking Vegan*. A gag gift from Holt on their thirtieth birthday.

Hawes smiled into his mug. "Does that offend your Italian senses?"

"More than you will ever know."

"If it makes you feel better, I've never opened it."

"Marginally." Dante circled the island, coming to stand in front of Hawes. "You were gone early this morning."

"Duty called."

"You left me here." He stepped closer and slid a hand over Hawes's hip. "You trusted me enough to stay in your condo without you."

"Iris is a good watchdog."

"So's your brother. The security system was armed. He'd know if I left."

Hawes shrugged and set his mug aside. "He'd know, but you were free to leave."

"You assumed I'd search the place?"

"You're a PI, aren't you?"

Dante returned his shrug with a smirk, which Hawes promptly wiped off his face with a kiss. The one he'd wanted in the dark of morning, for his own reasons. Reasons that were still tugging at Hawes's gut and other places south. He dove deeper into Dante's mouth, indulging in the taste of sweet cereal mixed with Dante's rich, mysterious flavor.

Dante matched his fervor, sucking Hawes's tongue in farther and tugging his shirt loose from his pants, unraveling Hawes's control while conversely stitching him together into the prince, who had additional reasons, other than just his desire, to keep Dante close. His vibrating phone was a well-timed reminder. He slipped out of Dante's arms and started down the hall toward the bathroom, leaving a trail of clothes in his wake. "I need to shower."

As Hawes had intended, Dante followed. "Can I get in with you?"

"Not if I'm going to make my meeting in an hour." He tossed his phone on the vanity, opened the glass door over the spa tub, and turned on the shower.

Dante pressed against his back, making Hawes dizzy with want. "You sure about that?" His hands snuck under the waistband of Hawes's boxers and pushed them down. They fluttered to the floor, and Hawes's cock jutted the opposite direction, begging for attention. Dante gave it to his balls instead, tugging. Hawes groaned and dropped his head back onto Dante's shoulder. Dante ramped up the torture, dipping his tongue into the crook of Hawes's neck and driving him wild. "Maybe I'd let you return that favor from last night."

Hawes rocked his hips, ass rubbing against Dante's erection, even as he did the math in his head, counting minutes and drive time. As much as he wanted to accept Dante's offer, there was no way he could make it work. Dante circled the base of his cock, and Hawes jerked out of his hold before it was too late. "No," he said, spinning. "You stay right there"—he pointed at the half wall across from the shower—"and answer my questions."

Dante did not look pleased, but he complied, hopping up onto the wall. Hawes stepped into the shower and turned the water to cool, tamping down his erection. "Did you know Walter Campbell?"

"Fog City have you and your siblings to thank for that?"

Shampoo bottle in hand, Hawes stared at Dante blank-faced. "For what?"

"Walter Campbell committed suicide. It's all over the news."

"If the news said…"

Dante scoffed. "The court said he was innocent, which was also a lie."

"Well, then." Hawes closed his eyes and washed out his soapy hair under the showerhead. "It sounds like justice was served."

"Is that what you do now? Vigilante justice? The winery, the warehouse, Campbell."

Rather than answer and officially incriminate himself and his siblings, Hawes reverted to his original question. "Did you know him?"

"Other than from the trial coverage, no."

"What about anyone else in local politics or at the courthouse?"

"I have my contacts," Dante said. "Same as you all do, no doubt."

Hawes continued to wash while working his source for information. "You said someone is trying to unseat me. Are they trying to do that legally too?"

"What's this about, Madigan?"

"There's an investigation, under seal."

Dante hopped off the ledge. "That's not the tip I had."

"About that tip…"

"I showed you what I had."

Hawes washed off the last of the soap. "And yet I still don't know why you're here."

The shower door opened, and cool air rushed in. Hawes turned, meeting Dante's cold, hard eyes without the glass for a shield. "I told you why."

"Isabelle Costa." Hawes hoped his voice didn't tremble as much as his insides. "You said she mattered, but that's all I've gotten from you. Why have you inserted yourself into my life and family business, Mr. Perry?"

One of Dante's hands flattened on the glass, the other closed around the towel bar at the back of the shower, boxing Hawes in. Hawes expected his voice to be cold and hard, like his eyes, but it was soft and tender, guilty almost. "She helped me at a time when I wasn't in a good way. She didn't deserve to get gunned down in the street, by her boyfriend or otherwise."

"She didn't."

"She deserves justice too. That's why I'm here."

Hawes didn't disagree with Dante on either of those points. He shoved his hands and face under the shower spray, remembering that night again. The truth that varied from the official story. How the water had run red, then cold, his fingers raw and pruned by the time Helena had dragged him out. Three years later, Isabelle's blood was still on his hands.

"Hawes."

A different voice, a different time, and yet things felt all too familiar. Too connected. Except this time, he could do something about it.

He turned off the water and yanked a towel off the rack. "I need to get going."

"Can I go with you to this meet?"

Hawes shook his head and stepped out onto the bath-mat. "A new face might spook the buyer."

"Buyer?"

"For the prototypes," he said.

"You're selling the explosives?"

"The prototypes." Hawes held his gaze, and his cover. "The prototypes business, actually."

Dante's eyes grew wide. "You don't think that's motive enough for a disgruntled operative?"

Fair point. He'd been thinking in terms of his new policies generally, not this one specifically. It was another stream of income, another line of attack, cut off to his operatives. The possibility had to be considered. "In the current context, yes." Someone like Lucas might read this change of course as another example of Hawes being a "pansy."

For Hawes, it was simply valuing life.

"You're still going through with it?" Dante asked.

"It's our empire now—mine, Holt's, and Helena's—and this is how we've decided to rule it. The prototypes are too much risk. Too high a cost." Too high a body count, collateral and otherwise. "We're getting out of that business."

The kiss Dante laid on him then was different than any other they'd shared. It was slow and deep, not riding the edge of blistering desire they'd been skating the past thirty-six hours. A deeper emotion rippled under the surface, something warm that Hawes wanted to settle into for hours.

Or yank himself back from a split-second later when Dante thrust a gun into his hand. He stared down at the awful weight, made heavier by the conversation they'd just had. "What the fuck?"

"If you're not going to let me go with you, then at least take protection, in case things go sideways."

"I'll have Holt with me."

Dante closed Hawes's fingers around the pistol. "You'll have this too."

Hawes wanted to vomit. "I can't use this." He shoved the gun back at Dante. At the man's frustrated look, Hawes bent, hiked up Dante's pant leg, and took his knife instead. "Satisfied?"

Dante tucked the pistol back into his waistband. "You don't like guns."

"They kill too fast, without thought. It's too easy to make the wrong call."

Confusing Hawes further, Dante hauled him in for another kiss. This one, however, was gentler than the last. Lazy, unguarded nips and licks of the sort Hawes dreamed of having the luxury to enjoy with a partner someday. And fuck if he didn't have somewhere else to be. He reluctantly broke the kiss and rested his forehead against Dante's. "I have to go."

"I'll talk with my contacts at the courthouse," Dante said after a couple of breaths. "Let me see what I can find out about this investigation."

"Thank you."

"That's two favors you'll owe me." Dante stole another kiss, then stepped out of the way, clearing Hawes's path to the vanity, save for a smack to his ass. "I do plan to collect."

Hawes grinned over his shoulder. "I hope so."

ELEVEN

Hawes swung Holt's SUV into the parking lot of the run-down buffet restaurant and parked among the cars scattered across the lot. Ride-share commuters, according to the realtor who had the property listing. The owner was still making money off the site, which had been sitting on the market for years. He was making more than usual today with the fee Hawes had paid to use it. Less than a mile from their South San Francisco warehouse, and only a few from SFO, where their buyer was flying in, the deserted restaurant site worked well for their purposes.

In the passenger seat, Holt was scrolling through news feeds on his tablet, reviewing the press coverage of Campbell's death. By the glimpses Hawes caught of the suicide headlines, they were still in the clear.

The glimpses of his brother were a different story. Holt's decline into zombie-dom continued—darker bags under his tired eyes, his auburn beard shaggier, and his washed-out skin contrasting starkly with his colorful tattoo sleeve. Tattoos that stood out more vividly when unobscured by a baby in his arm.

Amelia had the day off and had taken Lily and Rose to visit Cal. Holt was jumpier without his daughter in sight, but it was safer this way. They weren't expecting danger, but it couldn't be ruled out. Helena was likewise absent, due in part to her job and in part to strategy. Whenever possible, they avoided putting all three of them in the crosshairs. One of them usually stayed back, as Holt had that morning and as Helena did now.

Hawes shifted, reaching into the back seat for the folder containing the sale documents and Holt's flannel. He dropped the shirt into his brother's lap. "Buyer's on time?"

"Landed twenty minutes ago." Holt tapped at his tablet screen. "And Lyft just ran his card. He should be here in ten."

Hawes snatched the realtor's keys out of the cup holder and spun them around his index finger. "Let's go on in." He rotated toward the door but was stopped halfway by Holt's hand around his arm.

"Wait!"

Hawes glanced over his shoulder. "There a problem?"

Holt's gaze darted all around, looking everywhere but at Hawes. "Are we sure we want to do this?"

"We?" Hawes twisted the rest of the way around to face his brother. "I'm sure. Helena's sure. Are you?"

"I don't want my hands in this any more than you and Hena do."

"Then why are you hesitating?"

Holt darkened his tablet, tossed it onto the dash, and slumped in his seat with a sigh. "The future."

"This is the future."

"There are so many unknowns, Hawes, and without this"—he nodded out the windshield in the general direction of their warehouse several blocks away—"it's another unknown. What if something happens to the cold storage business? Or to our other line of work?" He fisted his hands in his lap. "I still can't find the source of the leak about Papa Cal, who's dying. A PI shows up out of nowhere saying someone's out to kill you, and you can't keep your eyes off the guy. Brax has gone radio silent, and we're being investigated without knowing by whom or for what." His knuckles grew whiter and his breaths shorter, on the verge of hyperventilating.

"Hey, hey, hey." Hawes clasped Holt's arm, trying to shake him loose of the panic. "Breathe, little brother." And father… That had to be where this was coming from.

Holt confirmed as much when he relaxed his hands and lifted his fingers to his left pec, laying them over the water lily he'd had inked there after his daughter's birth.

"This is about Lily," Hawes said.

Holt leaned his head back and closed his eyes. "Mom and dad, our grandparents, they talked about legacy all the time, but I never truly understood until now."

"We all understand better with Lily in our lives. She's why we do any of this." To make a better, safer world for her, and to give her options, either in or out of the family business. But as much as she tugged on Hawes's mind and heart, he couldn't imagine the responsibility Holt felt. "That said, you're Lily's father. You and Amelia have the most at stake here. We all get that too. So if you want to call off this deal, we'll call it off. This only works if all of us are on board. That's how it's always been, and that's how it will always be."

"I'm sorry." Holt dropped his hand into his lap.

Hawes covered it with his own. "Don't be sorry. I'd rather you talk to me than bottle this up."

"It's been a lot."

"When's the last time you slept for more than three hours?"

Holt laughed, the sound exhausted and helpless, but thankfully without the earlier panic and doubt.

Hawes settled back into his seat. "What do you want to do here?"

"We go through with it," Holt answered without hesitation.

"Are you sure?"

"It's what's right." Holt straightened and reached for his tablet. "We have the trust fund for Lily."

"Mine too, if anything goes south."

Holt's gaze shot to him again; he looked stunned.

"Don't act surprised," Hawes said with a smile. "She's all our legacy. At least until she has to share it with more brothers and sisters. Or cousins," he added with a wink, then turned for the door. Holt didn't stop him this time.

Hawes stopped himself, however, when they were halfway across the parking lot, his mind snagging on something else Holt had said. "If you want me to tell Dante to get lost, I will."

Holt handed Hawes his tablet and shrugged into the flannel. "Not yet. He could be useful, and you like him."

"I do," Hawes admitted. "But our family means more to me. It always will." Any serious relationship Hawes had would only work if his partner understood and accepted all of him, family and businesses included, but that sort of full disclosure required trust. No guarantee. Not like the trust he had in his family.

Holt held out his hand for his tablet. "How is that fair to you?"

"It's not fair if I compromise any of you."

"Don't use us to push away every relationship." A flash of righteous indignation brought Holt's eyes to life. Hawes would take it, even at his own expense. "You have to trust someone."

"I trust you, Helena, and Amelia." Hawes grinned and clapped his shoulder. "We can't all be as lucky as you, Little H."

Holt covered his hand, holding it there. "If I could find a partner, if Mom and Dad did, if Papa Cal and Rose did too, then so can you and Helena." He squeezed Hawes's hand. "There's too much good in both of you not to share it with someone special."

Papers were strewn across the lone buffet table remaining in the cavernous shell of a restaurant. Disclosure packets, purchase agreement, grant deed, bill of sale, and the various other title and escrow documents required to transfer ownership of their warehouse. On paper, it would look like a simple real estate sale. In reality, what was inside the building on the property was far more valuable to Shawn Gillespie than the land or the building itself.

Gillespie and his two attorneys were flipping through the papers for a third time. Hawes didn't begrudge them their careful review, especially as the documents had not been emailed in advance. Too easy to disseminate and draw attention. And while the disclosure documents could have been sent electronically, the deed and tax documents had to be originals. Hawes would ferry the stack of signed documents to Helena, who'd file them at the end of the week, allowing Gillespie time to move out the inventory before the change of ownership triggered a building inspection and tax reassessment.

Hawes didn't mind the few days' delay. All he cared about was that the contents of the warehouse were no longer his inventory to move. They were officially getting out of the explosives business. No more using them and no more making them for anyone else either. Not when Hawes had no control over how they'd be used and who might get swept up in the collateral damage.

Like Isabelle Costa had been, albeit more directly.

Unbeknownst to anyone, Isabelle, a secretary at MCS, had been carrying on an affair with one of their operatives, Zander Rowe. According to an anonymous tip Hawes had received the night of Isabelle's death, Rowe, who was supposed to be transporting a truck full of explosives, was instead diverting it to the highest bidder, a domestic terror cell hell-bent on attacking City Hall. Hawes had raced out after Rowe, calling for backup but not waiting for it to arrive, too terrified for his city and his family's legacy. He'd caught up with the truck, and a gunfight had ensued between him and Rowe.

When a second person had climbed out of the truck's cab, pistol first, Hawes had fired on instinct, killing a woman whose only crime had been falling for the wrong man. A hostage who'd only been trying to protect herself. Hawes hadn't realized that until it was too late, when he'd knelt over her and seen her bruised face and mangled wrists. He'd failed to call out, so she wouldn't have known he'd won the shoot-out. She'd found Rowe's spare gun and was trying to escape. Hawes hadn't given her the chance.

Helena had eventually talked him down that night—one life lost to collateral damage versus the many more who likely would've died if that terrorist cell had gotten hold of the explosives, but that one life was too many for Hawes. The risk that a tragedy like that might happen again, that his own weapons could be used against his family or the city he loved, was unacceptable. He would've sold the explosives business the next day if he could have, but extracting themselves from existing agreements had been time-consuming, as had been vetting a buyer.

They'd found the right one, eventually. A real estate developer, Gillespie would be using the explosives for project demolition, not for criminal purposes. That said, he was getting a criminally good deal on materials and real estate, which made him willing to look the other way as to the explosives' origin. Except as Gillespie waved off his attorneys and began read-through number four, Hawes was beginning to wonder if his buyer was getting cold feet. This was not merely a careful review. If that were the case, Gillespie or one of his attorneys would have spent more time on the disclosures. Instead, Gillespie was hung up on the purchase agreement, staring at it with wide eyes and increasingly pale skin.

"Is there a problem?" Hawes asked from across the table.

Gillespie's eyes flickered up, then away, avoiding Hawes's gaze.

Tell one.

"No problem," Gillespie said. "Just making sure I understand everything."

Tell two.

Nothing in that standard form purchase agreement or the other escrow documents was out of the ordinary, especially for a developer who regularly conducted real estate transactions.

Hawes leaned back in his chair and crossed one leg over the other. "All the terms are consistent with our conversations."

"Yes, it's all here."

Beside Hawes, Holt held a pen out to Gillespie. "We'll sign after you."

Gillespie took the pen and spun it around his thumb. Once, twice, a third time.

Tell three.

The attorney closest to Gillespie cleared her throat. "If there's—"

"No, it's fine. I'll do it." Another pause, another spin of the pen, then Gillespie began flipping pages and signing. Quickly, almost as if he was forcing himself to do so.

I'll do it.

Tell four.

"What firm did you say you were with?" Hawes asked the attorney.

The other one, a man, rattled off a string of names Hawes recognized. A large West Coast firm with an office in downtown San Francisco.

"Your firm handled the China Basin redevelopment, right?" Hawes said.

"Yes," the woman attorney replied. "Years back now."

Tell five.

Hawes straightened in his chair. Next to him, Holt

tapped at his tablet. "Amazing to see how much the area's changed," Holt said. "When I was a kid—"

"There." Gillespie threw the pen down. "Your turn."

"A moment, please." Hawes stood and picked up the signed documents. "We just need to clear signing authority with our attorney."

Holt was already up and headed for the far end of the room. He held out his tablet to Hawes, a text open from Helena.

Wrong firm, she'd replied in response to Holt's inquiry regarding the China Basin legal work.

"That's what I thought," Hawes said, voice low.

"Those attorneys are on the firm's website, but they could have hacked that, or asked the firm to change it for a day."

Hawes glanced back at an impossibly paler Gillespie. "Something's off for sure."

"'I'll do it' was a dead giveaway."

"Signaling us?"

"If those attorneys are actually law enforcement, and they told him who we were, who do you think he's more afraid of?"

Even if Gillespie didn't know they were assassins, he did know they had access to explosives enough to blow him and his buildings to bits. Leverage like that did tend to work in their favor, especially when law enforcement officers, by contrast, could leverage a target only so far, given the bounds of the law.

"They don't have probable cause to raid the warehouse," Hawes said, connecting the last of the dots. "They need him to purchase it to gain access."

Holt nodded at the papers in Hawes's hand. "And our signatures to prove we owned the building and trafficked the explosives inside it."

"Let's not do that." Hawes folded the papers in two. "We haven't done anything but discuss a sale of real estate so far. We can walk away."

"I think that would be wise." Holt darkened the screen of his tablet and tucked it under his arm. "Competing offer?"

"Works for me." Hawes led them back across the room. "I'm sorry, but we're going to have to cut this meeting short."

Gillespie shot to his feet. "All you have to do is sign."

"Your money will be wired immediately after," one of the "attorneys" added.

"There's another offer," Hawes said. "A better one."

"I'll match it!" Gillespie countered.

"That's good to know. We'll consider all our options and be in touch. Now, if you'd please." He held an arm out toward the restaurant door, beckoning them to leave. "The owner's realtor for this building will be here in five to collect the keys."

"Madigan, please. Let's make this deal."

"I'm sorry, Shawn," Hawes said, meaning it. He hated to think what the feds had on Gillespie to put that kind of desperation in the man's voice.

And what about what they had on him? Not enough to make a move, but enough to connect their activities to the warehouse. To the deal they'd brokered for its sale. Was this connected to the investigation Campbell had mentioned?

In any event, their investigation was stymied for now, or

at least this play was. Recognizing defeat, Gillespie's escorts ushered him out, and Hawes closed the doors behind them.

"Find out what they have on him," he said to Holt, who was gathering the rest of the papers on the table. "Make it go away."

"He tried to set us up."

"You saw him. Did he look like a man with options?"

Holt grunted in acknowledgment and shoved the papers into their folder. He lifted his eyes, and they were more than a measure concerned. "It'll be viewed as weakness if word gets out that we let him do this to us without consequences."

"He didn't do anything. I think, in the long run, we'll get more out of saving him than damning him."

Holt didn't look convinced, but further argument was forestalled by Holt's ringing tablet, Amelia's face lighting up the screen.

"Hey, babe," Holt answered. "What's up?"

"You need to get to the hospice house," she said. "It's time."

Hawes jostled through the lingering lunch crew in the hospice house kitchen and bolted out the back door, desperate for space and air. He killed people for a living, but the last three hours, watching his grandfather die, had been utter hell. Counting the seconds between Papa Cal's last breaths, the tears running down Rose's face, the number of times Helena tapped her nails or how often Amelia and Holt handed off Lily, each of them needing the extra comfort in turn. Not to mention the twelve times Hawes had had to sign his name on the termination-of-life papers. How many more documents would he have to sign this afternoon? Funeral arrangements, corporate formalities for MCS, the list went on.

Hands laced behind his head, he stalked through the rows of the small backyard garden. His long legs ate up the distance in a few quick strides, but the high privacy walls hid what he didn't want the rest of the world to see. His own shortened breaths, his own tears, the number of times he drummed his fingers against his skull. He needed to get his shit together before he stepped out the front door a different man than when he'd entered.

Sweat dripped down his spine as he paced. The morning fog had burned off early, gracing San Francisco with a rare sunny summer day. Fitting for the last day of Cal's life, a man whose existence swung wildly from light to dark. Local businessman and beloved Pac Heights fixture during the day, the last man you ever wanted to see headed your way at night.

And fitting for the moment Hawes wasn't sure he was ready for.

A coronation by sun rather than his beloved fog.

The screen door squeaked open and banged shut behind him. The sound of footsteps didn't follow, but Hawes knew he wasn't alone. He lifted his right arm and waited for his sister to slide in under it.

Sure enough, a sniffling Helena snuggled up to his side and wrapped her arms around his middle. He hugged her close, and they stood like that for several long minutes, until Helena loosened her hold and walked over to the stone bench under the garden's sprawling plum tree.

"Thank you," she said as Hawes lowered himself next to her. "For always being able to do what none of us can."

Hawes curled his fingers around the front edge of the bench's carved seat. "What does that say about me?"

"That you're the strong one." She covered his hand between them. "You always have been."

"Don't discount yourself, Hena."

She cracked a wobbly smile. "You remember how Papa Cal used to practice saying my name with you? Mom and Dad loved to tell that story."

Hawes chuckled. "Every day until I got it." Cal would sit him down with a piece of paper—Helena's name written out phonetically on it—and use his heavy silver pen to tap out each syllable. Holt didn't need a lesson, he got it on the first try, but it had taken Hawes a year longer to work out that middle syllable. By then, the nickname had stuck.

"And the day you finally got it? Tell me the rest."

How could Hawes forget it? His grandfather had been so happy and proud. Not at all disappointed that it had taken Hawes so absurdly long in the first place. He'd called Noah and Charlotte back from the office, Rose down from the second floor with Holt, and Cal had repeated it over with Hawes, clapping and cheering when he got it right. "He went to Eastern in Chinatown and got a box full of those mooncakes I loved so much."

"Those things were the best. When was the last time you had one?"

Hawes racked his brain. "I can't remember."

"We should fix that." Helena bumped his shoulder. "Soon."

"I'd like that." Hawes lifted his arm and tucked his

sister back against his side. "Maybe Rose would too, after a bit."

Helena ducked her chin, staring at her hands that had taken up their nail tapping again. "Can you imagine ever loving someone that hard?"

The image of Dante stretched out on his couch, book on his chest, Iris at his feet, jumped unbidden to Hawes's mind. He shook it off, unwilling to contemplate love in relation to a man he hardly knew. Attraction and lust were there for sure, as was that strange steadiness Dante provided, but love? Not quite so instantly. Not when loving and trusting the wrong person could spell disaster for Hawes and his family.

"Me neither," Helena mumbled, interpreting his silence as a no. Hawes didn't like the dejection in his sister's tone.

"Holt manages," he said.

"He's the brave one. You're the strong one."

"And you?"

"To be determined. I just can't imagine…" She cleared her throat. "To lose your other half like that, I'm not sure I could risk it. Maybe I'm the scared one."

"Maybe I am too," Hawes admitted.

Helena had it wrong. Their grandmother was the strong and brave one. She'd sat at Cal's side, crying but never letting go of his hand until Amelia had confirmed he'd taken his last breath. And even then…

"She wouldn't look at me," Hawes whispered.

"She wouldn't look at any of us."

"What if she doesn't forgive—"

"Don't go there." Helena wrapped both her hands around his arm. "She wanted you to hold the health care power of attorney because she too knows you're the strong one."

He sure as hell didn't feel like the strong one right then. Unsteady, uncertain, reluctant. All better adjectives for the jitteriness inside him. The fact that he knew exactly what —*who*—he needed to steady him, troubled Hawes all the more.

TWELVE

I went ahead and let him in.

The text from Holt pinged as Hawes reached the front steps of his building. Just in time to stave off the swell of disappointment at not finding Dante waiting out front for him.

Because he was waiting inside.

Hawes realized it wasn't wise to depend on this man he hardly knew, but after the day he'd had—from Campbell's ominous warning, to the explosives sale gone sideways, to his grandfather's death and the fifty-nine times Hawes had had to sign his name since—he needed someone else to be the steady one for a little while.

He needed to let go after white-knuckling the oh-shit handle all day long.

He'd had his moment of weakness in the garden with Helena, but then he'd pulled it together and been the strong one they'd needed, doing his job as eldest child and official head of the family businesses. Rose was settled back at the house with her cats and Lily, funeral arrangements were in motion, and Amelia, Holt, and Helena had been fully briefed on the day's events.

Hawes was dead on his feet and dead inside. Dark to dark, he'd gone with barely a breather, the only bright spot the brief exchange with Dante that morning. He'd kill for that shower together now…

But dinner, it seemed, was first on the agenda tonight. The rich aromas of sesame oil, soy sauce, and chilies wafted down the hall, reminding Hawes that in the chaos of his very long day, he'd forgotten to eat. And reminding him of his conversation with Helena. Of his grandfather, who was now gone.

The pink box of pastries on the coffee table brought the memories on stronger, a tsunami that forced Hawes to brace a hand on the nearest pillar. "Who told you?"

Dante looked up from where he stood behind the kitchen island, emptying takeout cartons onto plates. "Your sister." He blindly tossed a crispy shrimp to Iris, who was stalking the tops of the cabinets on the kitchen side of the loft wall. "Since I was in Chinatown, I swung by my favorite place for the rest. You hungry?"

Yes, said his brain, but he couldn't get the word out past the lump in his throat, drowning as he was in comparisons between this day and the day his parents died. He'd had to make the call that day too, and afterward, he'd brought Holt and Helena home from the hospital, cooked them breakfast, and tucked them into bed. Only once they were asleep had he retreated to his bedroom and screamed into the pillows. Alone. After he'd taken care of everyone else.

Unlike that day seventeen years ago, he wasn't alone tonight. Dante was in his kitchen, dishing out food and treating his cat. Taking care of him. It was domestic, it was different, it was welcome, it was everything Hawes wanted, and his gut clenched in hope and fear. Was this—*Dante*—his chance at what Holt and Amelia, his parents, and his grandparents had enjoyed? A partner who got it, who understood and accepted what he did, and stood by his side? Who'd help him protect his family and the empire they'd built? But only until Dante found out what happened to Isabelle. Then Hawes figured he'd be staring down the barrel of his gun instead. He might finally get what he wanted, only to lose it, because that's how his luck had been going lately. Hell, most of his life.

"Hey, Madigan, where'd you go?"

Hawes blinked, surprised to find Dante no longer in the kitchen but standing right in front of him. He stared into those bottomless brown eyes—wonder, hope, and dread a paralyzing cocktail.

Dante lifted a hand and coasted it over his jaw. "You with me?"

Hawes blinked again, shaking himself from the daze, and turned his face into the offered warmth, nuzzling Dante's palm. "Thank you."

"I'll take that as a yes to the hungry question."

"I'm sorry. I'm just—"

Dante cut off his words with a quick yet thorough kiss that left Hawes panting and pressed between the pole at his back and Dante's hard body against his front. "Don't apologize for anything tonight," Dante murmured. "Feel what you need to feel."

Hawes wanted to feel more of Dante—the bare biceps under his hands, the silky hair tickling his cheek, the hard thigh between his legs—but he also wanted to wash away the day and feel clean. And judging by the embarrassingly loud grumble of his stomach, he also wanted to feel full.

Dante chuckled, the sound rumbly and sexy, and Hawes was tempted to tell hygiene and his stomach to go to hell, but then Dante stepped back and turned him toward the bathroom. "Go rinse off, and I'll have everything ready when you get back."

Hawes couldn't argue with that plan. Ten minutes later, when he came back into the living room, the kitchen lights were low, the Giants game was on, plates of steaming food were spread out on the coffee table, and two place settings were set up in front of the couch, a bottle of beer next to each.

"This okay?" Dante asked from where he sat on the couch. "I wanted to see the end of the game, but we can move to the dining—"

"This is good." Hawes fluffed the damp top strands of his hair, then bent a leg under himself and sank onto the cushions next to Dante. "Perfect, actually."

Dante handed him a beer and gestured at the food. "Pick your poison."

"Bit of everything would be great." Hawes took a swig from the bottle, the pilsner cold and refreshing. "I'm not too picky when it comes to food."

"Could tell that from the cookbooks. You've got everything from slow cooker favorites to fine dining."

Hawes shrugged. "The haute cuisine books are mostly there for the pictures, though I've tried a few of the simpler recipes. Sauces and the like." He wedged the beer bottle between his legs and took the plate and chopsticks Dante handed him. "You know as well as I do, growing up in a city like this, every food and cuisine is out there to try.

Whenever I found one I loved, I wanted to make it myself. Cal gave me my first cookbook on my eighth birthday. He bought me the last two months ago, on my thirty-third. Or I suppose Rose did, but regardless, I have them all still."

"Did you ever want to be a chef?"

Hawes washed down his bite of Szechuan beef with a swallow of beer. "I flirted with the idea, but I also enjoyed afternoons at MCS with my parents. I wanted that too. I liked that our family had its own business."

"And the other business?"

"Honest to God, by the time Cal sat me down and explained it all, I was just happy to know that my parents, who'd been gone a month then, were coming home, and that they weren't dead or getting a divorce. I couldn't figure out why sometimes one was gone and not the other, or both of them together, for long stretches of time. Knowing the truth, a lot of things finally made sense."

"How old were you?"

"Twelve."

Dante's mouth opened—he wanted to say something, make some judgment—but he held his tongue, or rather occupied it with noodles instead and turned his attention back to the game. During the next commercial, he loaded up his plate with seconds. "Tell me about him, Papa Cal, and not the stories everybody knows."

Hawes lowered his chopsticks. "I don't want—"

"Trust me." Dante slid back into the cushions beside Hawes. "It'll make you feel better."

Hawes wasn't so sure about that, but the box of pastries on the corner of the table was an easy story he could share. Each story after that became easier, telling them between bites of fried shrimp, spicy beef, noodles, and then mooncakes. How Papa Cal had painstakingly restored every element of the Pac Heights house, and how Hawes's mother had spent hours with Cal, laying the entryway's mosaic tile, piece by piece, ultimately winning him over. How he'd regularly taken each of the grandkids to the office to see how the business was run. How, until the past few years, he'd taken Rose out to Tadich Grill every year on the anniversary of their first date. Then how Rose had brought the meal to him, once he'd been unable to go out anymore. How memory would flit through his eyes during those moments.

The stories went on, long past the food and the game, and what emerged was the picture of a patient, loving man when it came to his family, his friends, the waitstaff at restaurants, the neighbors up the street, the employees at his company. A counterweight to the quick, swift death he doled out in the shadows, that made him and the Madigan name feared in certain criminal circles. It was a balance, Hawes realized, one he was trying to recreate for himself and their family, albeit in a slightly different manner.

Dante reached out and brushed back the hair that had fallen over Hawes's forehead. "You know what you're going to say for the eulogy now?"

Hawes gaped at him. "How'd you know?"

"Who else would it be? You're the one who holds it together." His hand drifted down to cup Hawes's cheek. "I'm getting the sense you always have been."

"Doesn't feel like that." He closed his eyes and rested the weight of his head, his world, in the palm of Dante's hand. "Almost everything that could go wrong today did."

The statement begged the question, and Hawes expected the investigator to ask it. Instead, Dante curled his hand around Hawes's neck and drew him closer. "Well… then let's make something go right."

Right was Dante's mouth on his, deep and searching like their kiss that morning. Right was Dante gently pushing him back into the cushions so he could straddle Hawes's lap. Right was Hawes's hands touching every part of Dante he could reach. Over his hard chest and broad shoulders. Along his strong bearded jaw. Through the long strands of hair Hawes released from Dante's topknot, a curtain of brown waves falling around them.

Hawes could have stayed like that for hours, kissing and touching, except that their rolling hips reminded him of another something that would be oh-so-right. "I owe you a favor," he mumbled against Dante's lips. He slipped a hand between them and grasped Dante's erection through his jeans.

Dante grasped his wrist and pulled Hawes away from his prize, pinning his hand to the couch cushions instead. "This is about what you need tonight."

"I need this." Hawes thrust his hips up, his erection through his track pants nudging Dante's. He didn't care how needy he seemed, how desperate. If Dante was offering, Hawes wasn't holding back. He'd walked in here tonight feeling dead inside, but with Dante on his lap, kissing up and down his neck, he was burning up. Alive. He did not want that fire to go out. He clenched Dante's hand, drawing his smoldering gaze. "I need to taste you," Hawes said with another roll of his hips. "I want to return the favor."

One side of Dante's mouth ticked up. "All right, not gonna argue that offer." He climbed off Hawes's lap, pushed the coffee table back with his bare foot, and stripped without preamble or modesty.

Dante standing naked before him gave *sexy* a whole new meaning.

Honest to God, Hawes didn't know where to look. The long legs and powerful thighs dusted with dark, wiry hair. The miles of ripped torso and fucking eight-pack abs. The light sprinkling of hair at the center of Dante's chest—even broader out of its tank—or the line of hair that ran from his indented belly button, down his pelvis between cut hip bones, to the dark patch of hair around his erect cock. A ruddier tone of olive, it was thick and long, with a vein running up one side and moisture pearling in the slit. Scratch that, Hawes did know where to look. The same place he wanted to taste. His mouth watered.

"Like what you see?" Dante rumbled above him.

Stripping off his tee, Hawes slid to the edge of the couch and spread his legs on either side of Dante's. Head tipped back, he shot Dante an incredulous look. "Has anyone ever said no to that question?"

"Not since high school."

Even then, Hawes doubted that once a person got a look at Dante's cock, they'd care overly much about his lanky limbs or then-unbalanced features. Teenage Hawes sure as fuck wouldn't have cared. As far as Adult Hawes was concerned, all those now-balanced, handsome features were window dressing compared to what he wanted right here, to the man Dante was proving to be. Except maybe the hair, which Hawes was rather attached to already.

And while he couldn't reach the long strands on Dante's head from where he sat, Hawes could treat his fingertips to the springy hair on his legs, to the muscles in his powerful quads, to his firm, round ass cheeks. He cupped Dante's generous backside, hauled him forward, and shoved his face into the crease between thigh and groin. Intoxicating, the powerful, musky scent tinged with a hint of eucalyptus body wash. Dante personified. The guy who rode a Harley, always had a book on him, looked and strutted like a rock star, and carried a pistol, knife, and cuffs. A mystery.

Hawes flicked out his tongue; the mystery tasted even better than he'd imagined. Fuck, he could live right there. Could forget everything and drown in Dante. In the smell, taste, and heat of his skin. In the blood thumping in Hawes's own ears, and in the two points of pleasure and pain dominating his present existence—Dante's cock brushing his cheek and his own achingly hard dick trapped in his pants.

Fingers wove softly through his hair. "You with me?" Dante asked again, voice both gentle and rough.

"Can I stay here?"

"Sure, but fair warning, you're gonna get come on your cheek in another minute or so."

That didn't sound so bad, though what a fucking waste. Hawes tilted his head back and raked his gaze up Dante's flushed torso. Power and desire surged through him at finding Dante's face equally heated. "Can't have that," Hawes said with a smirk.

Dante's answering laugh morphed into a moan as Hawes tongued the underside of his cock. He closed his lips around the head and sucked it into his mouth, the smell and taste of Dante kicked up a thousand. Wanting more, Hawes relaxed his throat and swallowed as much of Dante as he could before triggering his gag reflex. He fisted the base of Dante's cock to make up the difference and began working him over, savoring every ridge his tongue skirted over, every bead of tangy precome that tickled his taste buds, every one of Dante's moans that echoed in his ears. They grew louder, the thrust of Dante's hips more urgent as Hawes trailed a hand over Dante's ass, fingers sneaking into his crack to tease his hole. Hawes wanted to push inside, desperately, but the supplies he needed to make this good for both of them were in his room.

Not that this wasn't already amazing.

Dante gently squeezed his scalp, not directing but enough to get Hawes's attention. "You have boxers on under those track pants?"

"Nuh-uh," Hawes grunted around his cock.

"Pull it out. Jack yourself."

Best idea ever. Using his hand that was already slick with spit, Hawes shoved down the waistband of his pants and took hold of his cock, groaning in relief.

A shudder rippled through Dante, and his cock inside Hawes's mouth grew harder. "Get there, Madigan. Hurry." His hand slipped out of Hawes's hair and down his neck, lightly grasping his nape like a collar.

Hawes pressed into it, reveling in the added support and the rhythm Dante set for them. He sucked up and down, in time with his own fist, speed ratcheting up in intervals until he couldn't hold back his release any longer. Come spilled over his fingers, sticky and warm, and he groaned out his pleasure around Dante's cock.

"Ah, Christ," Dante cursed, body curling over Hawes's, both hands landing on his shoulders.

He needed Hawes to return the favor, to steady him, and it was enough for Hawes to stave off the oncoming postcoital fog. He just needed to push Dante the rest of the way over the edge, and then they could drift there together. He cupped Dante's balls with his come-covered hand and tugged. Dante thrust forward with a shout, coming over Hawes's tongue and down his throat. Salty, pungent, hot— all the flavors of Dante in one potent mixture. A mystery Hawes could happily spend years solving.

THIRTEEN

An increasingly familiar sight greeted Hawes the next morning. Holt and Helena were milling around his living area while Dante made himself at home in the kitchen. After getting a surprisingly good few hours of sleep, Hawes had left Dante snoring on his couch in the wee hours of the morning. Once awake, Hawes was doomed to tossing and turning, and he didn't want his insomnia to doom Dante too. Or his nightmare mumblings to unintentionally reveal the truth about Isabelle's death. He'd retreated to his bed to starfish on his own, until Holt had texted a half hour ago to say he and Helena were headed over. Hawes had gotten up to do his business. Dante too by the looks of it. Hair up in a loose bun, he was dressed and at work behind the stove.

"Is this also becoming a thing?" Hawes said from where he stood at the other end of the island, admiring.

Dante grinned back at him. "They're not trying to kill me this time."

"Not yet, Mr. Hair," Helena said as she claimed a barstool.

"Play nice," Hawes chided. He gave her a peck on the cheek, then made a beeline for the coffee maker.

Dante passed him in the narrow space, and Hawes instinctively lifted a hand, fingers itching to trail over Dante's back. But with his siblings in the room, he wasn't sure how they or Dante would react.

Dante answered the question for him, stealing a quick kiss on his way back to the stove, bag of shredded cheese in hand. "You'll need to make more coffee." He cut a look to the dining table, where Holt was typing furiously on his laptop. "Someone drank the first batch."

"Yes, please," Helena chirped from her stool, voice at odds with her narrowed, assessing eyes. She definitely hadn't missed the brief exchange.

Coffee before deadly sister. Hawes moved Dante's book clear of the machine, refilled it with water and fresh grounds, and pressed Brew.

"Rough night with Lily?" Hawes called to his brother.

"Rough night all around." Holt finished typing, then shifted to straddle the bench. "Got her down about an hour ago. Grandma's watching her. She seems to be one of the few things that brings Rose some comfort too."

"And Amelia?"

"Hospital. She thought it was more important to take time off for the funeral tomorrow and through the weekend."

For better or worse, Papa Cal's declining health meant funeral arrangements had been on standby. Hawes just had to sign the papers and give them the go-ahead yesterday. Everything had come together quickly.

The coffee maker beeped right as Dante flipped off the stove. "Mug's waiting for you on the table. Take that on over"—he nodded at the coffeepot—"and I'll be right behind you with the food."

Hawes peeked around him. "What did you make?"

"Egg scramble out of what you had in the fridge." He sprinkled the shredded cheese liberally on top. "Didn't have time to bake it into a frittata."

"This weekend?"

"That could be arranged. You'd owe me another favor."

"I'm good with that." Favors worked out well for both of them. Hawes grabbed the coffeepot with one hand and trailed the other over Dante's lower back as he'd wanted to do earlier.

Helena didn't miss that exchange either. She slid off her stool and matched Hawes's stride across the living room. "This is all very domestic." Assessing for sure, cautious too, which in a way, Hawes was glad to see after her defeated manner yesterday. This was the sister he knew.

"You told him about the mooncakes," Hawes said.

"You needed someone last night." Empathy eclipsed her vigilance, but only for a second. "Keep your guard up."

Definitely getting back to her usual self. And she was right. He couldn't let hope for a future he'd thought impossible make him complacent.

"You gonna stand there with the coffee all day or pour?" Holt said, holding out his mug for a refill.

"Are you sure you need one?" Hawes replied. "Or do you want to crash for an hour on the couch?"

"Nap sounds good, but we need to go through all this first." A mess of scattered folders and papers were spread between the four place settings.

This did not look paperless. "What is *all this*?"

Dante set the cast-iron skillet down on a trivet at the end

of the table and began dishing out eggs. "While you all were dealing with matters yesterday, I did some digging."

"Why didn't you tell me about this last night?" Hawes asked.

"I mentioned that I was working on my end of things. But the details were not what you needed then."

The instinct was there to argue, which was good, but it was better that Dante had waited to tell him. Now he was clearheaded and ready to tackle whatever this was. "Did you find out anything about an investigation?"

"Nothing recent."

"What did you find?"

"Several avenues of investigation were opened five years ago." Dante handed him three folders. "Health department, SFPD, and ATF." The usual suspects, given their various enterprises. "They went nowhere at that time. Ditto three years ago when investigations were reopened. The timing in both cases can't be discounted."

"When I stepped in for Cal," Hawes said.

"And after Isabelle's death," Dante added.

"They were looking for a way in," Helena said.

"Likely," Dante said. "If they'd found anything, they would have tried to use it against you. See if you'd bend or break."

Sausage, peppers, and eggs didn't taste so delicious anymore. Hawes forced down a bite with his coffee. "They wouldn't have gotten anywhere."

"I went back into the computer logs from then." Holt rotated his laptop so Hawes could see the screen. "Multiple pings and attacks. We shut it down—they didn't get through my firewalls—but someone was trying."

Hawes glanced at Dante. How much to disclose in his

presence? The PI had been digging, he knew what they did, and he was still here, helping them. They'd be at cross-purposes soon, but at this juncture, they'd gain more by Dante being in on more of the story. Across the table, Holt seemed to reach the same conclusion, his eyes flickering to Dante, then to Hawes, followed by a nod.

"Okay, but all these investigations were in the past." Hawes nudged the folders with his mug. "Campbell said he saw a folder on the judge's desk *last month*. Why would the judge have any of these out?" He turned to Helena. "Did it sound to you like he was talking about an old case?"

"No," she answered. "I definitely got the impression it was current."

"Maybe one of the cases was reopened," Dante said. "Someone who thinks they can get to you another way, for a different reason."

"Cal's declining health."

"But you've been in control for five years."

"And all of a sudden I'm being challenged internally too."

Helena nudged the files back in his direction. "Maybe because an insider knows about these."

"The meet yesterday," Holt spoke up. "You said it yourself, Hawes. If we'd signed those documents and turned over the property…"

"And if Gillespie had given them access to it…" Hawes propped his elbows on the table and scrubbed his hands over his face. "Fuck, and I was trying to move the proto-types out of the organization."

Helena grasped his wrists and lowered his hands. "*We* were, and obviously, someone doesn't like that."

Didn't like how he was handling the organization at all.

"Whoever it is, were they trying to eliminate me so the investigation didn't proceed? Or were they the tipster?"

"Doesn't matter," Helena said. "You're gone either way. Even if Madigan Cold Storage goes away, our other associates won't. They'll just reform under a new leader."

All because he wanted to do things right. "I'm trying to make things better. Cleaner. So there's less chance of collateral damage, less chance of an investigation. I'm trying to stop another—" Isabelle Costa. He cut himself off from saying her name aloud, not willing to go that far yet with Dante in the room.

"By eliminating the most lucrative part of the business," Holt said, wisely skipping over Hawes's near slip and reiterating his point from yesterday.

Hawes bolted up from the table, cursing.

Dante caught his wrist. "You're not gonna like what I say next."

"Seems to be a habit too."

"Not always," he said with a smirk. That crooked smile, together with the sure hold around his wrist, reined in Hawes's rising agitation. Until his next words. "I don't think you should go to your grandfather's funeral."

"But the eulogy. You helped—"

Dante squeezed his wrist. "I didn't have the whole story."

"Hawes—" Helena started.

Hawes brought his other palm down on the table, hard enough to rattle the dishes. "Absolutely not. The last thing I'm going to do is show weakness. And I won't disappoint Rose." He straightened, and Dante released his wrist. "Besides, didn't we begin this week with the idea of flushing out the traitors?"

Holt gulped. "At Papa Cal's funeral?"

"Hopefully not. Of course I don't want it disrupted, but either way, we're done with this bullshit," Hawes declared. "This organization is ours now. No one is going to take it from us."

"One of you has to stay behind," Dante said. "In case an attack does occur at the funeral."

Hawes and Helena spoke at the same time. "Holt."

"Why can't it be Amelia?" their brother protested.

"You need to be the one with Lily," Hawes said. "Out of all of us, your hands are the cleanest. You have the best chance of staying with her." Hawes walked around the table and held his brother's face in his hands. "You two are our legacy. I'm not letting anything happen to either of you."

FOURTEEN

Amelia turned from the front windows and straightened her black dress. "The cars are here."

Holt, dressed in jeans, tee, and a flannel, scooted to the edge of the chair where he sat with Lily. "Are you sure I can't go?"

Beside him, Hawes brushed his fingers over Lily's head. "You need to stay here, for her." He hated asking his brother to skip their grandfather's funeral. Papa Cal and Holt had been close. After their parents' deaths, Holt had floundered, and it had been Cal who'd suggested he enlist rather than go to college. It had been the right call. Holt had found his purpose, and the benefits were still paying off. Hawes could never thank Cal enough for that guidance. What he could do was protect Holt and his legacy. "We talked about this."

"I know. I just—"

Amelia laid a hand on Holt's shoulder. "I'll stay too."

She didn't look any happier at the prospect. Of all of them, she'd been closest to Cal. He'd recruited her ten years ago, a young nurse who hadn't blinked at his injuries when he'd turned up in her ER. She didn't blink either when he'd asked her not to call the cops. She'd been their on-call nurse from then on, and once Cal learned what she could do with pressure points—and with a troubled Holt when no one else could reach him after he'd returned home from the service—Amelia had been welcomed into the family. Then last year she'd given them the greatest gift of all: Lily.

Holt shook his head. "Grandma needs you."

Rose had seemed weaker since Cal's death, not unexpected when one lost their other half. Amelia had kept close watch, as she had over Cal.

"And with you there," Holt added, "I will be too." He dipped his face to kiss her knuckles.

The quiet comfort they shared made Hawes's chest ache. Ninety-nine percent of the time he was happy for his brother, but in that one remaining percent, jealousy always reared its head at the most inconvenient moments. He walked over to the window and braced his arm on the intricate casing. He wished the man out there, behind the wheel of Holt's SUV, was in here with him. He considered sending a text to ask for an update. Anything to reestablish the connection, to call up the steadiness that, over the past day of making plans for this one, had eroded. Had deteriorated further overnight as he'd stayed here with his family rather than with Dante.

Hawes reached for his phone but was diverted by the *tap-tap* of cat claws and the *click-clack* of high heels on the stairs. With the cats in the lead, Helena was on her way down with Rose on her arm. Hawes met them at the bottom of the stairs, and his grandmother, for the first time since the night before Papa Cal passed, lifted her face and met his eyes.

Her blue ones, the same icy shade as his, were weary yet determined. She'd done her grieving, and now she was ready to move forward. She'd been the same after Hawes's parents' deaths. Torn up privately, until it was time to present the public face of the family. She'd been Hawes's best teacher in that regard.

"You'll honor him today." Not a request—a demand.

"I'm ready." Because Dante had helped him get there.

"Good." She shifted from Helena's arm to his. "You'll do him proud."

Hawes's relief was palpable. Rose's approval mattered more to him than anyone's now. Cal's expanding ventures would have failed if not for her tireless efforts at making the social and political connections they needed to succeed, on both fronts. There'd be no legacy without her either, and while Hawes and his siblings were changing the way things were done, he didn't want her to think he was ruining or disrespecting everything she and Papa Cal had built.

On their way out, they stopped by a tormented Holt and snoozing Lily, Rose giving each a kiss on the cheek. Hawes did the same, kissing the tops of their heads, then escorted their grandmother outside, where July was back to normal in San Francisco. Cold and foggy. They took the stairs slowly, and at the curb, Rose insisted he ride in the town car with her, Avery at the wheel. Helena and Amelia would ride in the car ahead of them, Zoe driving. Hawes had figured Rose would want Amelia or Helena with her, but as long as he and Helena were in separate cars, they were keeping with the plan.

The plan that had Kane in an unmarked cruiser across

the street, popping caramels and keeping an eye on Holt and Lily, and Dante in the SUV behind the two town cars. Hawes caught Dante's gaze in the rearview mirror. Brown eyes held his, and Hawes let the steadiness he'd missed wash over him. The next few hours didn't seem so daunting.

St. Patrick's had been packed for Papa Cal's funeral. It seemed all of Pac Heights had come down the hill to the giant red-brick cathedral where Hawes's grandfather had worshipped his entire life. Since safety concerns had forced them to forego the separate wake and graveside service, everyone who'd wanted to pay their respects had attended the service and waited in the receiving line after, their numbers spilling out into the church's courtyards. An hour after the service had ended, there were still people milling around his grandmother at the church's side doors. Off a bit from the crowd, Hawes rested against the metal rail at the bottom of the steps and surveyed the scene for anything amiss.

"So far so good," Helena said as she descended the steps. She leaned next to him and covered his hand. "The eulogy was beautiful."

"Thank you." Hawes ducked his chin, but only for a moment, before lifting his eyes and scanning their surroundings again. "I wanted to do him justice, as our grandfather. I wanted them to see who he was to us."

"Thank you for doing that and for handling everything. Like you always do." She patted his hand. "We ask a lot, and we forget to ask if you're okay."

"I'm okay, promise." He bumped her shoulder. "Just tired and ready for this to all be over."

"I'm glad nothing happened to disrupt the ceremony."

Hawes was too. He wanted to flush out the traitors, but he also wanted to honor his grandfather in peace. They'd gotten that much. Now he wanted to get his family home safely and move on to securing control, once and for all.

"Call up the cars," he said. "Let's wrap this up and get back to the fort."

She nodded and pulled out her phone, while Hawes corralled Rose and Amelia. "I'm sorry to interrupt," he said, smiling politely at the few lingering neighbors. "But the cars are on their way around. Time for us to go."

They said their goodbyes, Amelia confirmed next week's burial of the ashes with the priest, and Rose took Hawes's arm again as they descended the steps. "You could have done that thirty minutes ago."

"I was trying to be polite."

"I'm too tired for polite." She gave him more of her weight as they crossed the square to where the two town cars were parked at the curb. "I just want to get home, get out of these blasted heels, and see my great-grandbaby. You'll ride with me again."

"Yes, ma'am." It was more personality than she'd displayed in months, a glimpse of his spitfire grandmother from before Cal's condition had declined. Hawes was glad to see that life coming back to her, even if she did sound bone-tired. He opened the back door of the second car for her, watched as Amelia and Helena disappeared into the lead car, then waited until Dante swung the SUV around behind them before sliding into the back seat next to Rose. "To the house, please," he told Avery.

"Shouldn't take us more than twenty," Avery replied as they eased into the light traffic. "We're ahead of rush hour."

Five minutes later, just over Market, past the Theatre District curve, and waiting behind Amelia and Helena's car at an intersection, the hit Hawes expected finally came, but not from the direction he'd anticipated. He was discussing dinner plans with Rose when their car was rammed—from behind.

"What the hell?" He twisted in his seat, glaring through the back window at Dante, who slammed into the rear of their town car again.

"What the fuck's he doing?" Avery hollered over a crunch from the front end. "He's pushing us into them."

Hawes whipped back around, glancing out the front windshield. The force of Dante's repeated hits was plowing their car into the back end of his sister's ride.

"He's waving his phone," Rose said.

Hawes spun, looking again out of the back window. Face fraught with alarm, Dante was thrusting his phone toward the windshield and shouting words Hawes couldn't hear as he continued to ram their car, pushing them forward, into the intersection.

"*Check your phone.*" That's what Dante was shouting.

Hawes dug his phone out of his pocket. The screen was lit with a group text from Holt. **Calls blocked. Car bomb incoming**.

Avery saw it the same instant Hawes did. A utility van shoving its way through cars, no regard for scraped paint or broken mirrors. Her foot moved from the brake to the gas. With traffic behind them, forward was the only direction they could go. Dante wasn't pushing them into the intersection. He was trying to push them through it. Before the van reached them.

"Go, go, go!" Hawes shouted, beating the back of the passenger seat.

In front of them, Zoe had gotten the same message and hit the gas, zooming the rest of the way through the intersection.

Behind them, Dante was pushing them out of the intersection and driving the SUV into the path of the oncoming van. Into the path of the bomb.

Oh God, no.

"We need to divert," Hawes yelled. "A different direction from Zoe. Get off the main streets." That was the best hope of drawing the van off Dante and minimizing collateral damage.

On the other side of the intersection, Avery broke left, and the van took the bait, swerving past Dante and onto a parallel side street, matching their direction and starting a game of block-by-block hopscotch. They stayed ahead of the van, just barely, thanks to Avery's driving skills, but they were going to run into traffic again soon.

Hawes's phone vibrated in his hand. **Bring him up Shannon. Trap**, read the message from Helena.

He gave the order, and Avery aimed them that direction, now herding the van. The van took the bait, thinking it was getting ahead. Avery gunned the engine, pushing them fast up Leavenworth, passing by the nose of the van at the intersection of Post and Jones. Then Avery hung a hard right onto Shannon, the back end of the car fishtailing.

The van's tires squealed behind them, but it righted at the last second, chasing them down the narrow alley. Hawes held his breath through the intersection at Geary, car horns blaring all around them. They made it through, the van still on their tail. As they cleared the first set of buildings, a flash of blonde appeared on the left. Helena, gun in hand, stood on the hood of the town car at the mouth of a parking lot. Then on the right, brown hair and denim, Dante taking a similar position in front of the SUV, in the lot on the other side of the street. Avery sped through the trap, and Hawes twisted in his seat, watching as the van did not, Helena getting its tires on one side, Dante the other. The van swerved and toppled over, glass shattering, metal scraping concrete, twisting and turning until Hawes could see the undercarriage.

And the timer and trigger attached to it.

0:05 in bright red digits.

Not enough time.

He banged the back of the passenger seat again. "Go!"

Hawes took one last look out the back window—watched his sister catwalk over the top of her car while Dante hauled ass the opposite direction, each of them taking cover in their respective parking lots—then dove forward, taking his grandmother down to the floorboard with him.

The blast behind them threw their car into the air, and gravity ceased to exist.

FIFTEEN

Sixty-two.

Hawes turned on his heel at the nurses' station and started back the other direction on lap sixty-three.

Helena stopped him halfway, nails digging into his biceps. "Enough, Big H. You're gonna wear a hole through this hideous floor."

"You think I'm the first person to pace this hallway?" He tried to wrench his arm free and failed. His sister's hold was expertly positioned to exert more pressure the harder he tried to escape. He shot her an annoyed glare and tapped his toe on the linoleum. "Floor's still here."

"Then take it easy on me. The circling is making me woozy."

He lowered his heel, and his ire, and studied his sister. She'd washed up after they'd arrived at the hospital, and with her makeup gone and damp hair in a bun, the week's strain showed on her pale, dainty face. Dark circles under her eyes, a deep groove between her brows, freckles that stood out more prominently across the bridge of her nose. He'd neglected to ask after her too. "Fuck, Hena, how hard have you been going this week?"

She let go of his arm and sank into the nearest bright-orange chair. "I've been working every contact I have on our shit, managing Brax, and also trying to move matters at work. I don't want to leave any clients in the lurch if we have to scramble."

Helena's legal work involved acquitting the wrongfully accused. If Helena ghosted on her clients, it could mean the difference between life and death. Hawes couldn't begrudge them or her that, otherwise all his efforts to minimize collateral damage were for naught. No innocent lives lost, period.

He lowered himself into the chair next to her and threw an arm around her shoulders. "I'm sorry. I should have asked sooner."

"You've been going hard too. All of us have."

"And yet you still saved my ass today." He kissed the top of her head. "Thanks for that."

"Thank Mr. Hair. He came up with that trap plan."

Hawes squeezed her tighter. "He wouldn't have had to if I'd listened to him in the first place."

Wouldn't have had to put himself in the path of the charging van or in the blast radius with the rest of them. Dante had been the first to reach them after too. He'd helped Avery out of their tipped car, and then the three of them had extracted an unconscious Rose and handed her over to Amelia to treat until the paramedics arrived. He and Dante had shared a single smoke-tinged kiss before fire trucks had come barreling down the alley. They'd only exchanged a few words and texts since, Dante staying on the scene while Hawes rode with Rose, Amelia, and Helena to the hospital. Where their grandmother now lay unconscious in a room across the hall.

"I made the wrong call and put all of us at risk. Maybe I shouldn't be in charge."

Helena drew back, litigator face on. "Don't be ridiculous."

But Hawes was on a roll, all the self-recriminations he'd banked tumbling out. "If I'd ceded power to you or Holt earlier, or hell, if I'd just stayed away today like Dante suggested, maybe there wouldn't have been an attack. Maybe our grandmother wouldn't be in there fighting for her life."

"Don't be so dramatic." Amelia stepped out of Rose's room and closed the door behind her. "She'll be fine."

"Is she awake yet?"

Amelia nodded, and Hawes shot out of the chair.

"Can I—"

At Amelia's quelling look, he shut up and sat back down.

"The doctor is checking her vitals. You can go in, one at a time, when he's done."

A baby's wail cut through the hospital noises, and Amelia was in motion before Holt and Lily even rounded the corner. They reached each other, and Holt wrapped Amelia in his arms, Lily between them.

Hawes forced down the wave of bile that stung his throat. "Fuck," he cursed low. "I could have taken her from them too."

"But you didn't," Helena said. "And you kept Holt and Lily out of the line of fire."

That didn't make Hawes feel much better. Neither did the dark look in Holt's eyes.

"Where's your guard?" Hawes asked before his brother could speak.

"At the crime scene doing his job." Holt handed Lily to Amelia. "He's on the warpath. Today could have been a lot worse."

Hawes expected no less from Kane. This was the very definition of tits-up. While they'd alerted him to a possible incident, the actual attack had been less contained and potentially more destructive than they'd anticipated. If that van had exploded near St. Patrick's or on a busier street, the body count would be much higher than just the driver. Hawes pinched the bridge of his nose, as if that would miraculously ease the headache pounding at the base of his skull.

"We need to talk." Holt's clipped voice was as dark as his eyes. "Someplace private."

"We can use an on-call room," Amelia said. She popped her head back into Rose's room, let the doctor know they'd return shortly, then led them into an unmarked room around the corner. It was a tight fit with the two sets of bunk beds and small vanity, but it worked for what it was lacking—no cameras and no listening devices.

Holt and Amelia settled on one of the beds, Helena on the other, and Hawes leaned against the door. "How did you know?" he asked Holt. "About the car bomb."

"We sent an operative to move the explosives out of the warehouse, like we talked about, while all eyes were on the funeral." Holt's face drained of color. "Except there weren't any explosives there to move."

"They're gone?" It only took a second for Hawes to

jump to the next logical, horrible conclusion. "They were going to kill us with our own bombs?"

"Some of them. The rest… We don't know where those are."

Not an inconsequential amount of firepower out there in God only knew whose hands. Fuck, this was the last thing they needed right now. "How was the building accessed without us knowing?"

"Someone's in my system. Alarms were deactivated, and there are multiple surveillance-footage gaps. I should have caught it sooner." Holt hung his head, skimming both hands over it. "I don't think it's anyone in my shop. I've triple-checked, and there are zero red flags. It's someone outside, but fuck if I can figure out who."

"How'd you link it to the van?" Helena asked.

"I was monitoring your cars the entire trip. You hit Market, and the van darted out like a shot." Holt hugged Amelia close. "Saw that too many times in the desert not to recognize it for what it was."

Hawes crossed to Holt's other side and clasped his shoulder. "You did good today. Thank you."

"It'll take Brax a few days to ID the driver by dental records," Helena said. "Can we do it sooner? Traffic or ATM cams?"

"Analyzing," Holt said. "And I'm looking for ghosts of the missing warehouse footage." He shifted his gaze to Hawes. "There's something else." That dark look had crept back into his eyes, and Hawes sensed he wasn't going to like what came next. "I'm not sure we can trust Dante."

Hawes stepped back and folded his arms. "Did you miss the part where he helped save our lives today?"

Amelia glared from her husband's side. "Hawes."

Holt, though, had enough anger for both of them. "No, I didn't miss that," he bit back. "Not a single damn second of it while Dante had me on the SUV's speaker as it was happening. He was the only one I could get through to."

Shit, Hawes hadn't known he'd been listening. He'd thought Holt had been in touch via the group chat only. He forced his hackles back down. "I'm sorry. It's just... He's done nothing to jeopardize us."

"That we know of," Helena said.

Holt continued before Hawes could reply. "I don't think he's working with the person trying to pull off this coup, but he still hasn't given us a good explanation for what he's doing here."

Hawes couldn't deny any of what Holt had said. He also couldn't deny he needed Dante. Needed his steady presence as everything else continued to unravel. Needed him most in moments when he didn't want to be the king. He couldn't do it twenty-four seven and keep his humanity. "Does it matter, if he's helping us flush out who that person is?"

"What if they're manipulating him too?" Helena said. "What if it's another way to weaken you?"

"You sent him to me the other night."

It wasn't a fair rejoinder. All bets had been off that night. She'd been trying to help him and had cautioned him again the next morning. He expected an icy response for his sharp retort, but she cast her gaze aside instead. Her shoulders slumped to match. "We all make mistakes."

"He *thinks* he's after what happened to Isabelle," Holt said, redirecting Hawes's attention from Helena's uncharacteristic concession. "That's his mission. It's stamped on his fucking card case."

"Wait. What?"

"I saw it in the restaurant footage from Sunday. 23:01 is stamped on one side of his leather card case. Isabelle's time of death."

"And you're just now telling me this?" Hawes nearly shouted.

Holt raised his hands, palms out. "Like I said, it's his mission. He's not hidden that from us, but I'm not sure who he's helping or who he's working for."

Hawes stiffened. "What else do you have?"

Holt withdrew his arm from around Amelia and stood. His massive form, unfolded, made the small room seem even smaller. "Brax ran the bullet from the alley Sunday night."

"Dante said it couldn't be traced."

"It was. To a federal evidence locker."

Hawes's heart skipped a beat. "Stolen?"

"Or accessed."

His heart skipped another beat, before his pulse kicked into overdrive. "You think he's a fed?" If Hawes had compromised them, he'd never forgive himself.

"There's no evidence of that, that I can find," Holt replied. "But how'd he get those bullets from a federal lockup? How did he get those investigation files? He's tied in."

"He's a PI, born and raised here," Hawes countered, grasping at straws. "He's bound to have connections."

"Or he's not who he says he is."

"What's that supposed to mean? He's not a PI? We have the licenses."

"I'm not sure if he's Dante Perry at all." Holt tapped at his phone a few times, then handed it to Hawes. It was the yearbook page they'd previously examined. "There's something wrong with that picture."

Hawes squinted and tried to see something other than the dark eyes, long nose, and angled jaw he'd come to know the past week. It was a younger version, but it was the same man. "That's definitely him. It's all the same features. He's not wearing any prosthetics to disguise them."

"I agree," Holt said. "But I could swear it's been altered. I'm having a hard copy of the yearbook sent to the house. I want to see it for myself."

Eyes closed, mind whirling, Hawes fell back against the door. He'd trusted Dante, more each day as this crazy week had gone on. Had he been wrong to do so? Was the future he'd begun to let himself hope for a figment of his imagination? Was Dante Perry?

Dante was waiting for him out front when Hawes returned to the condo. He pushed up from the step, tucked a folder under his arm, and fell into step beside Hawes. "What'd I do to piss off the gatekeeper?"

"Holt thinks you're a fed." No sense hiding the ball. Hawes had meant what he'd said earlier today. He was done with this shit, from all angles. "Or at the very least, that you're not who you claim to be."

Dante ran a hand through his hair and shook it out. Strategically so the thick fall of strands hid his face from the security cameras. No one, Holt included, could read his lips or hear him say, voice low, "And I think he's your traitor."

Hawes's bluster vanished, as did his breath. He

would've missed the next step if Dante hadn't wound an arm around his waist.

"Let's get inside," Dante said, "and I'll explain."

But by the time they reached the second floor and Dante closed the condo door behind them, Hawes had wrangled his surprise and was flexing his anger. One safety net after another had been ripped out from under him, and now Dante wanted to rip away one of the few remaining, one of the most dependable. He stalked into the living room and rounded on Dante. "Before you accuse my brother, explain yourself. Who are you?"

"Dante Perry. We've been through this. You've done the background checks. What did Holt find now to make you question me?" He tossed his folder on the dining table and straddled the bench.

Lower than Hawes and out of his direct path. De-escalation 101. Unfortunately, Hawes was way past de-escalation, too wound up from the day's events. "The bullet from the alley," he snapped. "You were wrong. It was traced to a federal evidence locker."

"According to Holt."

"According to Kane."

"Did you ask Kane?"

No, the chief had been too busy barking questions at him, but that wasn't the point here. Dante's deflection—his nonanswer—was. "Where'd the bullet come from?" he demanded.

"Pawn shop. Same place I got my gun. Guy threw the ammo in for free. Guess now I know why."

A plausible enough answer, but not the only thing that required an explanation. "Holt also thinks your yearbook picture is doctored."

Groaning, Dante covered his face with his hands. "Please tell me you did not unearth that thing."

Hawes stopped right in front of him. "Something you don't want me to find there?"

Dante dropped his hands, letting them dangle between his knees. A bright blush streaked over his cheekbones. "The worst years of my life, memorialized in print forever, and apparently now also digitized."

Hawes dug out his phone and opened the screenshot Holt had sent him. He shoved the device under Dante's nose. "That you?"

He took one look and glanced up at Hawes. "Of course it's me. Pinocchio nose and all. Right between the smoking-hot quarterback, Trey Palmer, and his girlfriend, head cheerleader Jenn Petrie. Let me tell you how awkward that was, passing their love notes back and forth in homeroom, sucking him off in the locker room after fifth period, then taking her to prom."

Hawes flipped the phone in his grip and slid the line of pictures left so he could read the names. He spread his fingers on the screen to zoom in. Richard Palmer III. Dante Perry. Jennifer Petrie. The names weren't visible before; Dante hadn't seen them. Hell, he'd barely even looked at the screen. Relief unknotted Hawes's shoulders, and irony sent a brow climbing. "Jocks and cheerleaders?"

Dante shrugged and gave him a half smile. "I was seventeen. They were hot." He lifted an arm, curled a hand over Hawes's hip, and tugged him between his spread knees. "Your brother is seeing ghosts. Or he's trying to put doubts in your mind to distract you."

The relief dissipated. "From what?"

Dante put his other hand on Hawes's opposite hip.

"From the fact that he wasn't there today. That the explosives went missing on his watch."

Unsteady, Hawes clasped one of Dante's forearms. "He warned us."

Dante drew him closer. "Scared you too, didn't it? Maybe into thinking you should step down?"

Hawes closed his eyes, recalling his conversation with Helena. That's exactly what he'd been thinking.

Dante gave him a gentle shake. "Look back at the past week. The botched deal with the explosives."

Holt had hesitated before the meeting, concerned about the hit to the family's income.

"The theft of the explosives by operatives Holt can't track."

The first time Hawes had ever known his brother to be stumped.

"Wiped electronic records, missing surveillance footage from the warehouse and the hotel in Big Sur, leaks about your grandfather's health, and the flash drive sent to me. There was never an inside or outside hacker, Hawes. It was the best hacker you already have. Holt Madigan."

The tip to Hawes the night of Isabelle's death.

"No!" Hawes protested, as much to himself as to Dante. "He's my twin. I know him better than anyone. I know how he thinks."

"Do you? Are you married, with a kid? Always the second? Never the prince, never the king?"

"Don't call me that."

"Your grandfather is dead. You are the king."

Hawes whirled away and laced his hands behind his head, pacing, as Dante carried on with the truth he didn't want to hear. Holt couldn't strategize how to win a card game. How the fuck could he do this?

"Did you think this was going to go easy? Power transfers rarely do."

Hawes dropped his arms and slumped against the nearest pillar, caught between wanting to run from these terrible ideas and wanting to curl up in a ball on the floor. Except Holt had always been his protector when he'd succumbed to the latter, all the way back to the playground. His fiercest ally. "He's never said anything..." Yes, he'd been worn down lately, maybe retreating a little, but Hawes had thought that was due to the very things Dante had mentioned. Lily. Amelia. Focusing on surveillance and digital assassination. "He's supposed to be the one who stays off the criminal grid. Clean. So he can always be there for Lily." The family's escape route, God forbid they ever needed it.

Dante stood, and approached slowly. "Did anyone ask Holt if that's what he wanted?"

No, but... "You've seen how he looks at Lily."

Eyes swirling with an emotion Hawes couldn't place, Dante lifted a hand and cupped his cheek. "He looks at her like he wants to give her the world. Like any father would. Do you know how he does that?"

Hawes turned his face into Dante's palm, hiding from the truth.

Didn't stop Dante from voicing it. "By being in control, and you've made sure he isn't a target for the cops. Not that he ever would be."

"Never," Hawes whispered. Not as long as Braxton Kane was the chief of police.

"There's more."

Hawes opened his eyes and winced at Dante's exponentially grimmer face. Like he'd been holding back the worst part. Hawes's stomach sank, but he had to know. He curled his fingers around Dante's wrist and drew his hand down. "Tell me."

Using the hand in his, Dante led him back to the table. He reached out and drew the folder to them, flipping it open.

Account records from an offshore bank Hawes recognized. Their family regularly did business there. "How did you get these?"

"Friend of a friend did a little hacking for me." He spread out the first three sheets. "Jodie, Ray, and Lucas did get paid."

Significant amounts, according to the highlighted records.

"By?" Given Dante's theory, Hawes knew the answer but needed to see the evidence for himself.

It was more painful than he'd imagined.

Dante pushed the fourth sheet in front of him. "All the deposits came from this account." Multiple entries were highlighted on the ledger. Dante drew his attention to the account holder's box. "You recognize the name?"

Tears pricked the backs of Hawes's eyes, and words fought to get out past the lump in his throat. "Holt's military call sign, and our mother's maiden name."

Dante curled a hand over his thigh. "There were two more payments of interest." He pointed to the most recent at the top of the page. "This one is to a trust fund for the benefit of Max Bailey's family. Do you know who he was?"

"The name sounds familiar." But Hawes couldn't place him.

"He was a platoon mate of your brother's. He's been in and out of mental health facilities since retiring from the army. PTSD."

That triggered the memory. "Holt was his peer support contact when Bailey returned home. What does he have to do with this?"

"Max Bailey rented a cargo van last night." Dante withdrew a photo from the folder. It was the same van that had been rigged to blow them up today.

"Oh God." Hawes pitched sideways, burying his face in Dante's chest. He didn't want to believe this. Didn't want to believe that his calm, quiet, devoted brother had manipulated a friend, someone who'd needed his help, into sacrificing himself. Didn't want to believe that he would sacrifice his family, his own wife, for control of the family empire.

"There's one more thing you need to see."

Hawes shook his head. He'd seen enough. He was coming apart at the seams—his empire, his family, his world disintegrating around him. There were no nets, just an endless free fall. He wanted it to stop.

Dante had other ideas. Hand around his neck, he drew Hawes upright, then turned over the highlighted bank account record. One line was highlighted on the back, an older transaction. "A payment was made to Zander Rowe, the day of—"

"Isabelle Costa's murder." Hawes recognized the date. It cut worse than the account holder's name on the front. "But all that was before Lily."

"And Holt's cleaning up the mess now, because of Lily. Securing the world, the empire, for her."

Hawes covered his face with his hands. Was it really

possible? Had his own brother engineered the worst moment of his life? Put him in a situation where he'd made an impossible choice and an innocent woman had lost her life? Soaked Hawes's hands in blood? "He wouldn't do that to me."

Dante's hand landed on the knot between his shoulders. "We all have a blind spot where family is concerned."

"No!" Hawes rocketed to his feet and shot out an arm, swiping the table clean. This wasn't a blind spot. This was his brother, his twin. He ran from the truth, nearly falling over the bench in his hurry to escape. He caught his balance on a tumbling lunge and stumbled into the nearest pillar.

Dante was at his side the next instant, looping an arm around his front and clasping his neck. Hawes wanted none of the steadiness he offered. Spinning meant maybe he could grab on to another explanation. Anything but the truth staring him in the face. Steadiness meant standing still and accepting that the person he thought he knew best in the world was the one he knew least.

He fought out of Dante's hold and circled the living room. "What the fuck am I supposed to do? I can't ki—" He cut off the heinous thought. "He's my brother."

"You bring him back in line."

"And my sister?" Helena had looked so stretched thin lately. Had she been helping Holt? "And Amelia? Whose side are they on?"

"We can't be sure."

Was that car bomb today only meant for him? Had he risked Rose's life by riding in the same car with her? She was awake when they'd left the hospital, would go home tomorrow if she remained stable overnight, but she would've never been there if not for Hawes, either because he was the target or because he made the wrong call. His fault, either way.

"I should have listened to you and not gone to the funeral. I keep making the wrong decisions. Maybe I shouldn't be in charge."

Dante stepped in front of him, blocking his path. "That's what he wants you to think. You are exactly the Madigan that needs to be in charge." Dante cradled his face with both hands. "You are the one that changed the organization for the better."

"*We* did it," Hawes said, staring at Dante through the tears pooling in his eyes, willing the other man to understand. "Me, Holt, and Helena. Who am I supposed to trust now? I can't do this alone."

"You don't have to." Dante brushed his thumbs over his cheeks, wiping away the wetness there. "Trust me. I'm on your side."

Would he stay that way once he learned the truth about Isabelle's death? Hawes doubted it, and then he'd be well and truly alone. Without Dante and without his family. He closed his eyes and leaned his weight against Dante while he still could. "I don't know how to do this."

Hand under his chin, Dante forced his gaze back up. The desperate flailing in Dante's eyes caught Hawes by surprise, but as quick as the turmoil appeared, it was gone, resolve hardening the swirling brown. "We'll figure this out, the two of us." Dante leaned their foreheads together. "But you have to trust me."

Hawes had to trust *someone*. Dante had his own agenda that would eventually make them enemies, but for now, he'd proved himself to be on Hawes's side. Maybe the only one left there.

"I trust you." He tunneled his fingers into Dante's hair and pulled him back, just enough to lock eyes. "Please don't make me regret it."

Dante kissed him, and regret was the furthest thing from Hawes's mind. As steadiness rushed back in, Hawes realized what he had to do.

SIXTEEN

Hawes felt more than a little guilty for tossing the past three hours of planning out the window. Guiltier still about the sedative he'd slipped into Dante's drink. Guiltiest of all about stealing his bike. But there was no way Dante would've let him do what he needed to otherwise, and without his bike when he came to, Dante would be further delayed. Hawes had bought himself an extra fifteen minutes, if not more. The hair-raising ride over was worth it.

"Where's Perry?" Helena asked from her usual perch above the drive, her blonde hair and Ka-Bar glowing in the lights from the house.

Hawes finished steadying the bike, then started up the stairs, taking his chances with the truth. "My condo. Passed out on the dining table."

Standing over Dante, chest tight, Hawes had gently pushed back the long strands of his hair and admired his handsome face, peaceful in sleep. Hawes did trust him, even if they'd only known each other a week. His heart was getting on board too, which was a dangerous first. Someone else he had to protect. But Hawes's heart and mind also trusted his brother, no matter the abundance of evidence to the contrary. Hawes understood why Dante believed it— the bank records and other connections to Holt were damn convincing. But not enough to turn Hawes against his twin. There had to be an explanation, and here was the best place to get one.

"He's still at your place after what Holt showed you?" Helena spun the knife in her grip. Hawes suspected it was as much a nervous tic by now as it was keeping her weapon at the ready.

Hawes sat on the ledge and lifted her bare feet into his lap. "He convinced me otherwise."

"What else has he convinced you of?"

"That someone is trying to tear apart our family."

The knife stilled in her hand. "Could it be him?"

"I don't think so. This started long before he came into the picture."

"But it escalated when he showed up."

"Or when it became clear Papa Cal was near death."

She cast her gaze aside, and in the quiet night, her gulp was loud.

"Chicken-egg problem, Hena."

"I don't trust him."

"You don't have to." He squeezed her ankle and waited for her eyes. "You just have to trust me."

"Do you still trust us?" She tightened her grip on the knife, as if bracing for pain yet also ready to dole it out, if that's what she had to do. She called him the strong one, but she was the glue that held them together, the one who asked the hard questions, and their family's best defender.

She didn't need to brace or defend in this instance. Never against him. "Always," he answered.

Her grip on the knife relaxed, as did the tension in her back, braced against the column. "Good." She lifted her feet out of his lap and swung them around to the tiled landing. "There's something you need to see."

He followed her inside and upstairs to Holt's lair. As he crested the top step, he faltered. One sweeping look and he wished he could unsee it all. From his crying brother in the corner rocker, Lily clutched in his arms, to the wreckage of computer equipment strewn across the floor, to the wall of monitors displaying the truth that had been hiding in all their blind spots.

He carefully stepped around the mess on the floor and inched closer to the monitors, struggling to believe, to understand, what he was seeing. Every image, every detail, struck like a bullet, tearing his battered insides to shreds.

Amelia entering the offshore bank, the logo over the door matching the logo on the account records Dante had shown him.

Amelia in the arms of a frayed-looking man dressed in army fatigues, the patch on his camo jacket reading: BAILEY.

Amelia meeting Jodie, Ray, and Lucas outside the hotel in Big Sur.

Amelia and Bailey at the warehouse earlier in the week, the timestamp matching a gap in the surveillance footage.

It wasn't Holt trying to pull off a coup. It was Holt's wife.

Amelia, who'd been recruited by Papa Cal, who had an eye into everything, and who could play cards with one look at her hand because she had an eidetic memory. Who was always looking over Holt's shoulder. The person in the best position to make it look like he was the guilty party.

"We found her print on one of the car-bomb components." Stepping out of the front alcove, blanket in hand, Kane moved behind a shivering Holt and tucked the knitted wool around his shoulders. "We don't know why she did it."

"Lily," Hawes said as he regarded his slumbering niece in her wrecked father's arms.

Dante had the motivation right, just the culprit wrong. The traitor in their midst was the other person who would do anything to secure Lily's future, including framing her own husband and stealing the throne.

Hawes turned away from the monitors and crossed the room to kneel in front of Holt. He brushed the fuzz on Lily's head and looked up at his brother. "She's safe, Holt. That's all that matters."

Tortured brown eyes lifted to his. "I'm sorry, Hawes. I should have—"

"This is not your fault." He lifted his hand from Lily's head to Holt's arm, clasping it tightly. "She fooled all of us."

"What's she after?" Kane asked. "What's her mission?"

"A seat at the table, officially. At the head of it."

"If anyone should have seen it, it was me." Helena tapped her nails, trying and failing to fight her own tremors. "She was so quick to come back to work, and when we'd talk, she was obsessed with the family holding power."

Power. To hold for Lily.

"That's what she cares about," Helena said, reaching the same conclusion Hawes had. She aimed a pointed look at Kane. "Not alliances." At Hawes. "Not any sort of code."

And finally her gaze landed on a heartbroken Holt, sympathy in her eyes. "Not even love."

Twin tears raced down Holt's cheeks as he held Lily closer. Kane readjusted the blanket around them and left his hands on the top of the chair, standing guard. Holt huddled with his daughter in the blanket, hiding from this awful new reality.

Hawes couldn't hide. This was his kingdom to protect now. He rose and turned to Helena, who was standing by the monitors. "Where is she?"

"Approaching your condo." She gestured at the surveillance feed showing the hallway outside Hawes's front door.

Hawes's earlier guilt came crashing back, a tidal wave compared to the earlier breakers. On the other side of that door was Dante, drugged and defenseless. Because Hawes had left him that way.

***

"Faster!" Hawes held on tight as Helena pushed the Harley harder, flying around turns and sailing over hills. For once, he didn't care about his own potential death-by-motorcycle. He was more concerned with Dante's potential death-by-sister-in-law.

They skidded to a stop around the corner from Hawes's building, out of sight and hearing range. Helena killed the engine, and Hawes toggled on the comm device over his ear.

"Kane, update."

While Holt recovered, the chief had taken over comms.

"I've got this," he'd said before they left. *"I'll monitor things until I have to call in the cavalry."*

Holt had spoken up then, misery in every syllable. *"Don't hurt her, please."* Gaze fixed on Lily, his Adam's apple bobbed as he fought to get the words out. *"She's her mother."*

"Give us a twenty-minute head start," Hawes had told Kane, then after a parting kiss to Holt's and Lily's heads, had raced out with Helena.

That had been fifteen minutes ago. This time of night, the streets were mostly deserted, making their ride through downtown fast.

"No movement outside the building," Kane reported. "Or outside your door."

But he couldn't speak to inside, which Amelia had entered with her thumbprint and code, one of the few other people who had full access. Hawes cursed his no-cameras-inside rule. His privacy was a small price to pay for lo—

Helena saved him from having to cut off his own dangerous thought. "How are we getting in?" she asked. "We can't just go up and knock."

Hawes had an idea, but it required Holt's assistance. "I need my brother," he told the chief.

"Hold on a second."

Muffled voices preceded a disgruntled wail from Lily. She quieted a moment later as Kane took up a horribly off-key lullaby. Hawes couldn't help but smile, circumstances be damned.

"I'm here," Holt said, and the flurry of keystrokes told Hawes he was in front of his computers.

Exactly where Hawes needed him. "We need your help."

"Let me guess. You need to break into your own panic

room." Holt's voice cracked, evidence of his earlier tears, but his deadpan sarcasm was back where it belonged.

Hawes smiled wider. "Twin powers activated."

"Knew there was a reason we bought that upstairs unit."

Technically owned by MCS, the condo above Hawes's was a blank box they rented out to artists as studio space and sometimes also used for shelter activities. Unbeknownst to renters, the locked "owner's closet" was actually a panic room for Hawes's condo below.

Holt had them inside it in less than two minutes.

"How do you want to do this?" Helena asked as she yanked off her boots. "Where do you think she is in the unit?"

"I'd guess either end of the main space so she can see the entire length of it, plus more weapons in the kitchen, but I can't see or detect anything through these walls. It's a panic room for a reason."

"Don't need it," Holt said. "I can use the Wi-Fi signals from your network and Amelia's phone to get her location."

"That sounds an awful lot like cameras, even if there are no pictures."

Holt talked over impossibly fast keystrokes. "I might have loaded some beta software on your router and in your smart-home-system app. I swear I haven't tapped it until now."

Hawes didn't totally believe him, but again, small price to pay in the current situation. And he'd latched on to a different, more important tactical advantage in something Holt had said. "Can you create a distraction using the app?"

Helena nodded, following his train of thought. "Kill the lights and blast the music when we drop through. I like it." She made a slicing motion with her hand by her ear—their signal for cut it—and flipped off her comm. Once Hawes did the same, she asked, "Can we do that and get her out alive? We promised him."

"That's my plan."

"Will Dante be on board with that plan?"

"Are you?"

Banked anger flashed in her eyes, but she shut it down just as quickly. "For Holt and Lily, yes," she said, resolved. She checked to make sure her gun and knife were secure. "But if I bloody her nose, can't be helped."

"No one will blame you." Hawes reactivated his comm and checked his knife and garrote were in easy reach. "Where is she, Holt?"

"Kitchen, according to the Wi-Fi."

"I go low, you go high," Hawes said to Helena. That had always worked well for them when dropping into blind situations.

She grinned and bounced on her bare toes. "Ready."

Hawes put his hand on the button next to the panic room door. "Cue the music."

"On my count," Holt replied. "Three, two, one."

Helena's "Go!" was the last thing Hawes heard before he slammed his palm against the button and the Ramones' "Blitzkrieg Bop" rent the air.

SEVENTEEN

The retractable door in the ceiling slid open, and Hawes dropped through, riding the soles of his Oxfords down the ladder rails into his living room.

He hit the floor, curled into a crouch, and Helena leaped over him. In the moonlight, she was a flash of black leather and blonde hair, practically walking on air as she took off from the middle rung, used him as a vault, and grabbed hold of the exposed overhead piping. She swung to the coffee table, landed graceful as a cat, then launched herself onto the couch, scampering up the cushions to the back frame.

Glass shattered from the direction of the kitchen. "Here!" Dante shouted over the music, confirming his position. "She's got a—"

Gunfire cut short the warning.

Hawes flipped up the coffee table, sending remotes, cookbooks, and Dante's paperbacks flying. Using the tabletop as a shield, he advanced, staying low, and Helena kept to higher ground, springing from couch arm, to barstool, to the kitchen island.

"Lights!" Hawes shouted to Holt at the controls.

The overhead track lighting blazed on, and the music dropped out. Hawes, at the end of the couch, dropped the table and grasped his knife. Helena stood on the island, knife in one hand, the other holding a gun trained on Amelia.

Their sister-in-law stood in the back corner of the kitchen, a swaying Dante in front of her, a gun pressed to his temple. "Sis," Amelia hissed, her green-eyed gaze locked on Helena.

While they squared off, Hawes took stock of Dante. Glassy-eyed, unsteady, hands tied in front of him. Even with her torture skills, Amelia was hauling him around more easily than should have been possible, given their height and weight differences. Noticing his attention, Amelia used her free hand to grab something off the counter. She tossed it at Hawes's feet. "You really shouldn't leave your pets home alone."

A syringe. She'd drugged Dante, on top of the sedative Hawes had given him.

Shit!

He glanced again at Dante, whose gaze kept wandering off him and toward the couch. Hawes thought it involuntary until Dante's left hand also twitched. Was he pointing at the couch?

"You gonna shoot me, sis?" Amelia said to Helena, her focus redirected.

Hawes used the distraction to sneak a look to the right and spied the butt of Dante's pistol peeking out from behind a pillow.

"You'd make an orphan of your niece?" Amelia taunted.

"She has a father."

Amelia pitched a flash drive onto the island, the plastic clattering on the granite. "All his crimes and yours." She cut her glare to Hawes. "All three of you. I send that to the FBI, and Lily won't have a father—or aunt and uncle—much longer."

"Why?" Hawes couldn't stop from asking. It had to be about more than securing Lily's legacy, if Amelia was willing to send Holt away too.

"Because we could be so much more, if you'd just take the fucking gloves off."

"I have no desire to start a war in my city."

"Our city. That's what it could be, Hawes. Who the fuck's going to beat the Madigans? Get your shit together, and the four of us can take what your grandfather built and make it even more powerful."

Power.

Helena had been right. This was what power looked like when it corrupted, when the desire for it went too far. He fucking hated that it had to be his sister-in-law who taught them this lesson.

"It's not about who we can beat," Hawes said as he inched closer to Dante's gun. He loathed the thought of using it, even for distraction. He hated the thought of turning it on Amelia even more. He'd promised Holt he wouldn't, but if it came down to her or the other two people in this room, Hawes would do what he had to. The kill, God help him, was vetted, but he had to try and bring her around first.

"It's about who we are, Amelia. Why we do what we do. For justice, not for money. *That* will make us more powerful," he said, appealing to her driving motivation. And to the other one too. "*That's* the legacy we want to leave Lily. Empires built on fear never last, nor do empires that kill the innocent, blindly or collaterally. That's not the empire or the legacy we want to leave Lily."

Amelia sneered. "Ever since that night—"

A flurry of movement erupted—Dante flinched, Amelia jerked him to the side, Helena stepped to the edge of the island—and for a split-second Hawes thought he was going to lose it all. "Wait!" he shouted, and everyone froze.

"Weapons down!" Amelia demanded.

Hawes dropped his knife and garrote at once. "Hena, stand down." He waited for his sister to lay down the gun and knife, to straighten with her arms and legs loose, ready to spring, before addressing Amelia again. "That night did change us," he said. "For the better."

"Gonna have to disagree with you." Amelia shoved the muzzle of her gun against Dante's temple, hard enough to make him wince. "You didn't handle it then, and now look what it's brought to our doorstep."

Dante clenched his tied hands. "Now, Hawes!"

Hawes lunged for the gun, ignored the bile rushing up his throat, and fired at the cabinet above Amelia's head, distracting her. Dante twisted away, wobbling precariously until he got his feet under him and swung his clenched fist up. He connected with Amelia's firing arm with enough force to knock her gun loose. He kicked it clear and shoved Amelia into Helena's waiting chokehold. Amelia went limp in seconds, her unconscious body hitting the floor a second after that.

That fast, it was over. That fast, Hawes realized it could have all been over for him and his family instead. As

Helena brought the butt of her gun down on the flash drive, shattering it in defense of their family, Hawes dropped Dante's pistol, a wave of unsteadiness taking out his knees. Dante was there, as he had been all week, albeit a bit wobbly himself. He looped his bound hands over Hawes's head and drew him into his arms, the two of them leaning on each other. "I've got you."

If there were earthly portals to hell, Hawes was certain the SFPD headquarters was one of them. Not that there was anything particularly hellish about the place itself. The shiny new building was spacious and modern, quite nice compared to other station houses in the city. Not nice were the looks Hawes was catching, especially from old-timers. Thinly veiled fear, outright loathing, and wary caution from the officers and detectives who'd come up during Papa Cal's heyday. They no doubt wondered how the Prince of Killers's reign would compare, given its bang-up start.

Curiosity was likewise a popular look among the younger set, officers who cut Hawes a quick glance as they passed by, or who openly stared at him from their bullpen desks. Hawes counted and tagged each one and mentally shuffled them into one of three buckets—too new to know better, still trying to make sense of the rumors, or on board with the Madigans' recent vigilante streak. He'd relay his observations to Holt next time they reviewed the SFPD's roster. Reactions and perceptions could be useful in the future, but given the option, Hawes would've skipped this visit altogether.

That, however, was not an option. Not while Kane interrogated Amelia in the room across the hall. True to his word, the chief had given them a head start, which put the cavalry on scene shortly after they'd subdued Amelia. She'd come to in the back seat of a police cruiser, and other than to confirm her identity and to answer yes to the Miranda warning, hadn't spoken. Hawes doubted she'd say anything more to Kane, but he had to wait to find out. Had to make sure his family was safe, even the one who'd betrayed them. He had to see this mess through to the end.

Helena appeared from around the corner with two coffees in hand. Hawes gladly accepted a cup, anything to battle back the cold chill and weariness creeping into his bones, a week's worth of sleep deprivation catching up to him.

"Heebie-jeebies, Big H?" Helena leaned against the wall beside him, as comfortable as she could be. Why wouldn't she be? Her day job required her to visit this and other station houses multiple times a week.

Hawes shivered at the thought and gulped more coffee. "I don't know how you spend so much time here."

"Not every accused criminal is guilty. Present case excluded"—she tipped her cup toward the interrogation room—"I like to think I'm better equipped than most to judge."

"Balancing out your karma?"

"You have your code, I have mine."

Hawes's chuckle was cut short by Kane emerging from the interrogation room. Through the open door, Hawes caught sight of Amelia, handcuffed to the metal table. Stone-faced and dead-eyed, she looked like a shell of her usual fiery self, even as she stared straight at him.

Kane closed the door, cutting off Hawes's view. "She's not talking."

At least there was that. He couldn't discount the risk of Amelia turning state's evidence—it would be another way to take him down—but she couldn't do that without taking the entire organization down, which had never been her goal. She'd wanted more power, but that was out of reach now. If she cared for her daughter, which Hawes truly believed she did, she'd want Holt free and clear to raise Lily with the family resources behind them.

Kane's hazel eyes landed on Helena. "She did ask for an attorney."

"Nope." Helena shook her head sharply. "Conflict of interest and she doesn't meet my criteria."

Hawes did laugh then, as did Kane, though the chief's amusement quickly turned grim. "Probably a wise decision. With her actions today and tonight, together with the evidence Holt and Dante collected and Amelia's prints on the explosives, we've got her for conspiracy to commit murder, attempted murder, kidnapping, and numerous financial and firearms charges. I don't see a convincing legal defense."

"Get her someone good," Hawes said to Helena, trusting she had the contacts to make it happen. "It's what Holt would want." It was what Lily deserved. Amelia was still her mother.

"You heard from him?" Kane said.

Helena laid a hand on his forearm. "He's fine. Lily was fussy for a bit, but he got her down. He seemed pretty distracted when I talked to him last, like he was on the trail of something else."

There was no shortage of disturbingly open threads: the whereabouts of the rest of the explosives, whether Amelia had more allies, how far back her treachery stretched, Dante.

"Where's Perry?" Kane asked, as if hearing Hawes's thoughts.

"Here." Dante rounded the corner. "Was getting my vitals checked and an IV push to flush the sedatives."

Something was off about him; Hawes noticed it immediately. The sedative was out of his system, but Dante's shoulders were stiff and his gait was more rigid than his usual casual lope. Then again, it had been an off night for all of them, and Dante had taken the brunt of the hits.

"Everything okay?" Hawes asked.

"Fine." Dante slid a hand over his lower back, and a measure of the steadiness Hawes had missed returned. "Except that part where I got drugged. *Twice.*"

Hawes cringed. He'd apologized on the ride over, but he understood if Dante was still angry, probably more so after giving his statement. "I'm sorry," he tried again, and got a stern, dark-eyed look for his efforts.

"We'll be discussing that later," Dante said, voice lowered.

Necessary, as their growing number was attracting attention. Noticing the same, Kane ushered them into his office and closed the door. "I need a straight answer this time," he said to Hawes. "Is this some sort of turf war that's going to bleed into my streets?"

Hawes wanted to tell him no, but he also didn't want to lie to Kane. That wouldn't be fair after all the chief had done to help them. "Apparently my way of doing things, *my alliances*, are not universally accepted."

Behind his desk, Kane ran a hand over his head. "Are you questioning those alliances?"

"Don't be obtuse, Brax," Helena said.

"Are you?" Kane pressed.

"You know where I stand," Hawes replied. "I'm taking my family's work in a different direction. There are bound to be detractors."

"You think it runs deeper than Amelia?"

"She recruited Jodie, Ray, and Lucas to her side. Tricked Bailey into helping her. I can't say for certain there aren't others. I assume that's what Holt is working on now. Assessing her reach."

Dante leaned a hip against the side of Kane's desk and filched a caramel candy out of the corner bowl. "What'll you do to the traitors?"

"Has anyone heard from Lucas lately?"

"Fucking hell, Hawes," Kane muttered. "I didn't hear that."

Hawes crossed his arms. "Hear what?"

Kane cursed and shooed them toward the door. "There's nothing more to do here tonight. Go home before you make a bigger scene of my station."

Dante pushed off the desk. "Keep us posted."

"And you do the same if things—"

"Go tits-up. Got it." Hawes waved a hand in the air as they filed out. "We're in the shit now, Chief."

Hawes shut the door on Kane's half groan, half laugh. In the hallway, Helena hung back by his side. "Give us a minute," she said to Dante.

Dante clicked the candy against his teeth. "I'll be outside."

Watching him go, Hawes worried again over his stiffer

than usual gait. Was he hurt or just tired? Or angrier than he was letting on about Hawes drugging him? About going rogue? Hawes put money on the latter.

"Don't think I have to ask where you're staying tonight," Helena said as they followed slowly after him toward the exit. "So tell me, is it a ten?"

"More like a twelve."

"I hate you," she hissed, but her small grin said *good for you*.

"I'll be by the house in the morning."

Hand on his arm, she stopped them by the stairs. Her grin vanished, all her typical catty bravado gone, weariness and concern dampening her eyes. "Please be careful. I can't lose any more family this week."

Hawes wrapped her in a crushing hug. "You're not gonna lose me, Hena. Not as long as you've got my back. Thank you for that tonight."

"Holt's gonna need us to have his too. Now more than ever."

"And we'll be there, for him and Lily."

"Good." She squeezed him tight, then drew back with a sly smile. "Enjoy your night with Mr. Hair and be home in time for breakfast." She kissed his cheek. "I'll put a pillow on your chair."

He rolled his eyes and started down the stairs, Helena's laughter echoing after him. He couldn't deny that the laughter and relatively normal, teasing exchange felt good.

Also welcome and good was the sight of Dante astride his Harley, waiting at the curb for him. "Your steed awaits."

"Thanks for not killing me for stealing it."

"We'll talk about that too."

Hawes had no doubt they would; he only hoped for

other nontalking activities first. He climbed on behind Dante and wound his arms around his middle, reveling in his solid presence. In the steadiness Dante provided. Hawes wanted more of that, wanted it all night long. "Take me to the castle."

EIGHTEEN

Hawes got as far as flipping on the hallway lights before Dante spun him by the arm and trapped him between the foyer pillar and his big body. Hand palming one side of his jaw, Dante dragged his tongue up the other, on his way to nipping Hawes's earlobe. Hawes failed to see the problem with being stuck between a rock and a hard place. Not a damn thing wrong with this. He tunneled his fingers through Dante's hair and encouraged him to keep going.

Taking cues like a pro, Dante swirled his tongue in the divot behind Hawes's ear. "You hurt anywhere?"

Hawes rolled his hips, dragging his aching cock, trapped behind layers of material, alongside Dante's, similarly straining his zipper. "Only one thing hurts right now." Fuck, he'd been hard the entire ride here. Cock pressed against Dante's backside, Hawes had been too distracted to worry about death-by-bike. Distracted by the abs he'd traced under Dante's tank, by the strands of windswept hair that had tickled his face, by the vibration of the bike between his legs, all of it stoking his desire. Seemed Dante's desire had been stoked too. Time to do something about that.

Hawes slid his hands under the collar of Dante's jacket and pushed it off his shoulders. "How are *you* feeling?"

Well enough to spin Hawes again, shove him face-first against the wooden pole, and jerk his suit jacket off over his arms. A protest was on the tip of Hawes's tongue, but it died with the thrust of Dante's cock against his ass. Turned into a needy moan when Dante yanked aside his shirt collar and sucked at the sensitive crook of his neck.

"Yes." Hand on the pole, Hawes canted his hips, and Dante's dick nestled against his crack. Exactly where Hawes wanted him. He wrapped his other hand around Dante's nape, keeping his face buried in his neck. The two points of contact were driving Hawes wild.

Then Dante added a third. Sneaking a hand around, he grasped Hawes's erection, taking layers of material with him as he slid his fist from tip to root. Hawes's braced arm gave way, and he collapsed onto his elbow.

Dante lifted his head in time to avoid a collision, but his hand around Hawes kept up the torture. "I'll feel better once I fuck you."

Now Hawes saw the problem. "Bed," he gasped out.

"Can fuck you just fine here." Proving his argument, Dante deftly unbuckled Hawes's belt, lowered his zipper, and slipped a hand inside his boxers. Another few seconds and he'd have Hawes's dick out and his ass bared, at which point Hawes would be a goner.

Summoning his last ounce of restraint, Hawes pushed off the pole and sent both of them stumbling backward. He rotated and clutched Dante's shirt, counterbalancing to keep them upright, and also keeping Dante an arm's length away. Steadier, he sucked in breaths while promising his dick and Dante, "Two minutes. I need to feed Iris and make sure everything out there"—he nodded toward the living area—"is secure. And since I'm going to pass out right after you fuck me, I'd rather it be in my bed than against the foyer pole."

Dante chuckled. "Fair enough." A flicker of some emotion streaked across Dante's face, killing the humor and dampening the heat.

"Hey, you okay?" Hawes moved to close the distance between them, but Dante sidestepped his approach, heading toward the living area instead.

"You're asking me that?"

"You were held hostage tonight, after being drugged twice."

Dante deflected again, looking around the living room, whistling low. "It's like it never happened."

"Madigan Cold Storage—both enterprises—cleans up after itself." Hawes skated his fingers over Dante's abs as he passed in front of him. At the *snick* of the cat-food lid, Iris bounded down from the loft. Hawes set her bowl on the floor and scratched behind her ears. She gave him a tail shake, then ignored his existence in favor of food. Straightening, he continued with his security checks. Balcony doors, check. Doors, check. Panic room, check.

"So the ladder to nowhere does go somewhere," Dante said.

"It does," Hawes said as he climbed down the ladder. "And you still haven't answered my question."

Dante stepped forward and caged him in, a knee between Hawes's legs, hands on the ladder rails on either side of his head. "I let myself be held hostage until you got here."

"You were drugged, for which I am sorry."

"I know you are," he said, voice softening. "And I know why you did it. Can't fault you for putting your family first. Just don't do it again."

Hawes nodded. "Thank you."

"As for being held hostage, I could've made a break for it."

"Why didn't you?"

Dante's gaze slid sideways, toward the kitchen, where chaos had erupted earlier. He opened his mouth like he was going to speak but shut it before words escaped. He refocused on Hawes and restarted. "It was your decision how to handle Amelia. You're the king now."

Hawes didn't think that was what Dante was going to say at first. He probably would have liked those words better. "Don't call me that."

"It's true."

"Tonight, I'm just the man who lost a dearly loved family member. The brother and uncle who is going to have to pick up the pieces." He grasped Dante's chin and drew him closer. "The lover who almost lost someone he cares about. A future he didn't think possible." Dante's eyes flared, and Hawes kissed him, quick and hard. "I'm just a man who could have lost everything."

Dante lifted a hand off the rail and cradled Hawes's face, thumb tracing the sharp hinge of his jaw. "You are not just a man."

"And neither are you." Hawes covered Dante's hand with his and coiled a leg around Dante's, trapping him close. "Don't ever sacrifice your safety for me like that again."

"I won't make that promise."

Hawes started to object, and Dante returned the earlier swift kiss. "Trust me in those situations to make the right call. I've earned that much."

Hawes's mind whirled as Dante captured his lips. He still had questions—Holt's and Helena's lingering concerns about Dante couldn't be disregarded—but no doubt, Hawes trusted Dante to handle himself when the shit hit the fan. He could use an ally, a partner, like that. And Hawes trusted Dante to handle him, especially tonight when other needs were so much closer to the surface.

Relaxing against the ladder, he opened wider for Dante's kiss, inviting his tongue to tangle with his as it swept inside Hawes's mouth. Dante tasted sweet, like the caramel candy he'd taken off Kane's desk, on top of the Dante flavor Hawes had come to enjoy so much this week —dark, mysterious, dependable. A favorite cocktail that filled Hawes's insides with steady warmth. That both ensnared and freed him. Dante's thigh between his legs, the rhythmic rocking of hips, his hard chest beneath Hawes's palms. The long, silky hair Hawes could wrap around his fist and hold on to. Or use to pull Dante back when it became clear, once shirts were shed and pants undone, that they were gonna fuck right there against the ladder if Hawes didn't move them elsewhere. Granted, the blowjob Dante had given him there ranked among Hawes's hottest sexual encounters, but it wasn't what he wanted tonight. "I'm not sure this is better than the foyer pole."

Dante fought his hold. "Picky, picky."

Tugging Dante's head back farther, Hawes licked a

stripe from his throat to his ear. "Fuck me in my bed," he whispered hotly, then released Dante's hair and trailed his hands over his shoulders to his biceps. "And let me fall asleep in your arms after."

Dante righted his head, wretched confusion swirling in his eyes, same as it had in the foyer. Hawes recognized the emotion now. He opened his mouth to ask about it, but Dante blinked it away the next instant. Desire returned, his dark eyes molten with hunger, and the instant after that, Dante shucked his pants and boxers. He pushed down Hawes's too, and as he stood he curled his hands under Hawes's thighs and boosted him into his arms. "Let's go, then."

Hawes flailed an embarrassing half second, unused to being so effortlessly manhandled, but then chagrin gave way to turned-the-fuck-on. He wrapped his legs around Dante's waist, cock delightfully nestled against warm skin and hard muscle, and looped his arms around Dante's neck. He drove his hands back into his long hair and attacked his mouth, trusting Dante to navigate to the bedroom despite Hawes's greedy kisses. His trust wasn't misplaced, his back hitting the bed in no time.

Dante came down on top of him. "Is this what you want?"

"Getting there." He kicked out a leg, taking Dante's knee with it, and braced a hand in the mattress, pushing up. Hawes rolled them so he was on top, but he was only there a second before Dante wrenched them the opposite direction. As they continued to wrestle, their slick cocks bumped and slid, limbs tangled, teeth nipped, and tongues licked, and the smell of sweat and precome filled the room. Hawes had never before grappled with a bedmate of equal strength and skill, and it was fucking exhilarating. By the time he finally got Dante onto his back, Hawes's knees on either side of his hips, his hands pinning Dante's to the mattress, Hawes was panting. His nipples scraped against Dante's chest with each breath, only making him more desperate to be fucked.

He glared down at Dante, daring him to make another move. "If I reach over to the table to get a condom and lube, are you gonna stay?"

Dante grinned and rolled his hips. "Risk you're gonna have to take."

Worth it, as were the consequences Dante delivered. Hawes had barely wrapped his fingers around the foil packet and bottle when Dante grabbed an ankle and flipped him onto his stomach.

"Tell me you want this," Dante said as he sat astride Hawes's thighs.

Hawes grasped the headboard rails and lifted his ass. "Yes."

Dante dribbled lube between his cheeks, and Hawes hissed at the cold. Dante chased it away with kisses dotted across his shoulders and fingers spreading the lubricant down his crack and around his rim. He pressed a thumb against Hawes's hole. "And this?"

"Fuck yes."

Dante's thumb pressed in, and Hawes saw the sun behind his closed eyelids. A bright burst of pain, then as his muscles gave way and sucked Dante in, a whole sky of stars came out to play. Endless and beautiful, made more so by Dante's fingertips teasing his taint.

A warm weight covered Hawes's back, Dante stretched over him. Hawes opened his eyes, and a curtain of brown waves fell around his face. "Christ, you're tight," Dante murmured behind his ear. "How long's it been, Madigan?"

"Too long." Fingers tightening around the rails, Hawes struggled between riding Dante's hand and humping the mattress for friction. "Need more, please."

Giving it to him, Dante worked him open until he was begging for his cock, wanting Dante inside him before he exploded. The rip of foil and snap of latex had never sounded sweeter. Even sweeter was the sound and sight— because Hawes had to look back—of Dante lubing up his cock, fist shuttling up and down his hard length. It was the most erotic thing Hawes had ever seen.

And the next second it was the scariest sight of Hawes's life. Stars became black holes, and Hawes came untethered, free falling with nothing but the bed rails and sheets to grab hold of. It had been too long. Years since he'd opened himself up like this—to the possibility of more than just sex, to a potential partnership, to making love with another man in his bed. With all that riding on the here and now, he needed more control.

"Sun—"

He didn't even finish the safe word before Dante shifted off and flipped him back over.

"Hey, hey, hey," Dante cooed, voice gentling. "I got you."

Hawes gasped out a giant breath, then sucked in a bigger one. "I'm okay, just need a sec, but stay with me, please."

"Not going anywhere." Dante straddled his hips, but not so tight or close as to be confining. Comforting instead. Same with his forearms on either side of Hawes's head, his fingers gently brushing back Hawes's hair while his own hair created a cocoon around them. Dante waited for his breathing to calm, then asked, "You still want this?"

"Yes. Want you inside me, together."

Dante lifted Hawes's hands and put them on his shoulders. "Hold on to me, then," he said, eyes burning with desire and understanding. "Hold on to me and let go, but only as much as you want to."

It was exactly what Hawes needed to hear, exactly the power he needed back, and with it came a swell of emotion that Hawes poured into the kiss they shared. Everything he'd never dared hope for, everything he never thought he could have. Until now. He dug his fingers into Dante's shoulders and held on tight, riding that hope as Dante slid into him.

Riding it higher with each thrust and roll of their hips, with each kiss stolen between quickened breaths, with each stroke of Dante's hand around his cock, until Dante snapped his hips hard one last time, their gazes locked, and Hawes exploded with him, as high on hope as he'd ever been.

NINETEEN

Light bloomed behind Hawes's eyelids, a sudden burst that pushed him from dozing to awake. For the sun to have broken through the fog, to be shining so bright that it poured through the windows and over the loft wall, it had to be midday. Fuck, when was the last time he'd slept so late? Probably the last time he'd been laid so well. Which was an understatement. Fucked into oblivion was more like it. Dante had been powerful, wild, and caring, totally in tune with him. Hawes had barely spoken his safe word, and Dante had adjusted. He'd given Hawes exactly what he'd needed.

And fuck, it had been good.

So good that Hawes woke relaxed and rested, eager for the day ahead for the first time in a week. There were loose ends to deal with still—pending investigations, missing explosives, imploding family—but today Hawes felt more like a king than he'd ever felt like a prince. Like he could walk out the front door and onto his city's streets with the same easy confidence Dante carried himself.

Or better yet, he could get fucked again first.

Eyes closed, he scratched his bare chest and stretched from the toes up, pausing when his ass gave a twinge of protest. He carefully bowed his back off the mattress, counting each vertebra as it bent. No pain there. He could make this work. He just needed to convince Dante. Hawes didn't think it would be too hard. Right arm above his head, he inched his left over the sheets, searching for the other warm body in his bed.

And came up empty.

Cool sheets. No Dante.

Maybe he was scrunched on the far edge of the king-size bed. Hawes did have a tendency to starfish when he slept. He moved to stretch farther and was yanked back—by cold metal around his right wrist.

He instinctively yanked at his arm, hard, nearly jerking his shoulder out of its socket. Eyes popping open, he arched his neck and spied one end of Dante's handcuffs around his wrist, the other around a headboard rail. The one Hawes had had his fingers curled around last night as Dante had...

Ah, seemed his lover had in mind the same start to the day as Hawes. Still in tune with him and what he needed.

A sly smile spread across Hawes's face, and his morning wood, already stiffening further at the memory of last night, plumped to full attention. He lowered his back and shoulders to the mattress and listened. Sounds drifted up from the bathroom. There was his lover.

"You know," Hawes called, raising his voice. "It defeats the purpose to cuff me to the bed, naked, and then leave. You're missing the good stuff."

The toilet flushed and steps thudded up the stairs, as if Dante had his boots on. Had he gone out somewhere?

Hawes inhaled deep. He didn't smell coffee or food, just the leftover musk of their lovemaking.

Before Hawes could enjoy another flash of memory, Dante appeared at the top of the stairs and robbed Hawes of thought. And all his breath.

Fully clothed, gun in hand, this Dante was not the same man Hawes had spent last night with, much less the past week. The top half of his hair was tied back in a ponytail, a holster was clipped to his hip, and his posture was rigid, as if those blips Hawes had noticed yesterday had taken root and grown into towering redwoods overnight. Worst of all were his eyes. They were all wrong. Not the molten brown Hawes had stared into as they'd come together. The fire in them was gone, snuffed out and replaced by cold, hard detachment.

Dante's voice was dead to match. "This exactly serves my purpose."

Dread settled like a boulder on Hawes's chest.

In his mind, Hawes replayed last night through a different lens. Was it possible he'd misread Dante's hunger, their flirtatious grappling, the passionate fight for and exchange of power? By the look of the stranger at the foot of his bed, the answer to that question was highly likely.

Shit.

Hawes tensed, preparing to reach across his body to the bedside drawer.

Dante, who'd become well acquainted with his reflexes —because fuck if Hawes hadn't goaded him into multiple displays of them—raised his pistol. "Nuh-uh-uh, I already removed the knife and panic button."

Hawes seethed. "I trusted you."

"You should have trusted your siblings."

Shit!

Holt hadn't been the only one suffering a blind spot. Hawes had been so eager for the steadiness Dante offered, for an ally and partner, for a life he'd written off as impossible, that he'd forgotten it was impossible for a reason.

Someone was always gunning for the king.

Silencing his naive hopes for more than thrones and empires, Hawes ignored his grieving heart and wrenched his mind into operative mode, evaluating exit strategies as he kept Dante talking. "Were you working with her?" he asked.

"With whom?"

"Amelia."

Dante laughed. It didn't sound amused at all. He stepped around to Hawes's side of the bed and stared down at him. Hawes yanked again at the cuff, testing the rail, and no longer comfortable under Dante's intense gaze, even if fire did momentarily flicker in those dark depths. "No, I wasn't working with her," Dante answered. "But she did tell me some interesting things before you and Helena showed up."

"Such as?"

"She was working for someone. Your throne's not safe. And my mission's not complete."

Hawes paused in his assessment of escape routes to unpack those three deceptively simple sentences. There were obviously more loose ends than he'd accounted for, but what struck Hawes most was Dante's use of the word *mission*. Tactical, in the same way his ex-army brother and Chief Kane often used it. Committed, in a way that spoke to abject devotion, above all else. Above any feelings Dante might have developed for Hawes.

"Your mission?" Hawes asked, every hair on his body standing on end.

"To bring Isabelle's killer to justice."

Hawes forced himself not to laugh. Not to cry. Isabelle's killer was right here, handcuffed to the fucking bed. Did Dante know that? Was that one of the interesting things Amelia had told him? Or did Dante remain in the dark about that most essential fact? Like Hawes had been in the dark about the most essential question Dante had dodged all week.

"Who was she to you?" Hawes asked again, sensing he'd finally get the answer and that he wouldn't like it one damn bit.

He was right.

Dante reached into his back pocket, withdrew a black leather billfold, and tossed it onto Hawes's chest. It landed open—to a gold-and-blue badge with a distinctive eagle on top. Hawes picked it up with his shaking left hand and confirmed his hairs had stood on end for a reason. "You're ATF?"

"Special Agent Christopher Perri."

Hawes flipped to the other half of the billfold, to the stranger's credentials, and read the truth for himself. Holt had been right. The digital copy of the yearbook had been altered. The picture was the same man, and he'd be in the same alphabetical position in the class roster, only a letter's difference between his real last name and the one he'd used for his cover, but the first name… "Christopher?"

"My partner used to call me Dante. She thought it was funny, given my nose and the fact that I always had it in a book."

Hawes's gut clenched. "Your partner?"

"Isabelle Costa."

Don't stop now!
Continue reading Hawes & Dante's story in *King Slayer*!

For all the latest updates on new projects, sneak peeks, and more, sign up for Layla's Newsletter.

Reviews are an invaluable tool when it comes to spreading the word about great reads. Please consider leaving an honest review for *Prince of Killers* on your favorite review site.

Thank you for reading!

ACKNOWLEDGMENTS

Funny story about how this series came to be... I was cruising Wander's website for cover photos for a different project when I found the shot that will be the cover of Fog City 3. (Tease, I know, I'm sorry!) I was captivated. I had to have that photo. But then my rational author pal, Allison Temple, said, "Nope, you can't buy the pretties until you have a story to go with them." A week later, I had the series outlined, the photos purchased, and Fog City was officially a go.

So, first, thank you Wander, and models Patrick and Ryan, for providing such wonderful inspiration. Thank you Cate Ashwood for taking those photos and giving me dance-around-the-room moments every time I opened a cover concept email. Thank you to Allison, and the other two Mooseketeers, Erin McLellan and L.J. Hayward, for your encouragement, insightful beta notes, and all around good cheer. To Cory, Kim, Leslie, Kristi, Keren and Susan, your brainstorming, comments, and feedback were instrumental in getting my vision for Hawes and Dante onto the page. To overlord and PA extraordinaire Leslie Copeland, I could not have done this without you. Your knowledge, patience, and network are amazing, and I'm so so lucky and happy that I found you. And to Hailey, Lucy, May, Annabeth, Aimee, Macy, Charlie, and all the other wonderful authors who have held my hand and shared your time and wisdom as I tackled self-publishing, all my heartfelt gratitude.

And last but not least, thank you, *Readers*. Thank you for your support of past series, for taking a chance on this new adventure, and for all the joy you bring to my author life. I could not do this without you. And yes, I know you probably want to throw your e-reader after that last line, but I promise, stick with me, and it'll be worth it. The last line is already written!

ALSO BY LAYLA REYNE

For the most up-to-date list of titles and a helpful reading order, please visit www.laylareyne.com.

Dead Draw

Bad Bishop

King Hunt

Best Play

Redemption Inc.:

The Accidental

The Bounty

The Martyr

The Boss

More Romantic Suspense / Mystery:

What We May Be

Variable Onset

Soul to Find:

Icarus and the Devil

Jason and the Storm

Paris and the Reaper

Atlas and the Traitor

Table for Two:

The Last Drop

Dine With Me

Blue Plate Special

Over a Barrel

The Sweet Spot

Sigh of Relief

ABOUT THE AUTHOR

Layla Reyne is the author of *What We May Be* and the *Agents Irish and Whiskey, Fog City,* and *Perfect Play* series. She writes sexy, intense LGBTQIA+ romance featuring competent adults in kitchens, sports arenas, car chases, and other high-stakes situations. Whether it's adrenaline-fueled suspense, rival athletes, vampires and shifters, or love mixed with mouth-watering foodie goodness, queer folks finding happily-ever-afters is guaranteed.

You can find Layla online at laylareyne.com and at the following sites:

BB bookbub.com/authors/layla-reyne

f facebook.com/laylareyne

O instagram.com/laylareyne

d tiktok.com/@laylareyne

bsky.app/profile/laylareyne